MENAFTER10

CASEY HAMILTON

AMBLE
PRESS

Ann Arbor
2021

Amble Press

Copyright © 2021 Casey Hamilton

Amble Press First Edition: September 2021

Print ISBN: 978-1-61294-219-3

Cover design by TreeHouse Studio

This book is dedicated to the man who gave up everything and everyone he knew to move to LA, didn't make it in Hollywood, lived in a matchbox apartment, worked a nine to five just to stay alive and ultimately wrote a novel that somehow made it all worth it.

MENAFTER10

PROLOGUE

God's light wasn't available to guide its men-children through the dark of night. Instead, what lit the streets after the sun had set was artificial, subject to flickering on and off, changing its color, going completely out and never being bright enough to ward off all the darkness.

That didn't stop them, though. They had needs, the certain sort of needs that peaked at night, in the midnight hours, when the only people still up were the ones likely up to no good. So they prowled the city in these godless hours, trying to satisfy themselves in the bars and the bedrooms open to them when everything else was closed.

Night was dangerous as it was. Even more so for them, men traveling through a nighttime as black as they themselves were, seeking satisfaction in strangers. They were men who liked men—not loved, *liked*—and they were free to be so, openly. But being a minority within a minority in society was never an easy thing to be, either.

It helped that there were apps made with them in mind to assist with their needs of the night. MENAFTER10 was the most popular of these apps. It was advertised as "the app of choice for urban men seeking urban men." The name referred to the hours when it reached peak usage by these predominantly brown shades of men.

Because of the app, they had it easier than any gay man had ever had it before. Sex could now be delivered faster than a pizza. No charge. No tax. No fee. Black male anatomy was served for free.

MENAFTER10 was now worth millions, after only a decade or so since the male-seeking-male websites and chat rooms and hotlines of the time died so that it could live. And it, in turn, had improved this market by giving it mobility, which came in the form of a location-based app allowing men to be found and filtered.

There were powers that came with MENAFTER10 that could be used at any moment from any location at any time. Powers that allowed them to discard, to discriminate, to attack, to block, to filter out their flaws, to be as bold as they could be behind the comfort of an unverified profile that didn't even ask for a real name.

Anyone with the app was granted these abilities. And with MENAFTER10's soaring popularity within its unique demographic, they all were almost Zeus in a way, so long as they were signed in. Every user wielded virtual thunderbolts but with them being the only ones online, there was no one to strike them with. Mount Olympus wasn't Mount Olympus unless there was an Earth underneath it to look down on. There was no mortal lesser than them to exert their power on. There was only themselves. And so, in their erotic escapades, they threw this cyber strength onto one another with the abandonment of wild gods, even though they only had the bearing of man.

PART 1

CHAPTER 1

SHEA BUTTER IN THE SUN

Chauncey's dick was up and standing before he was. There was sleep still stuck in his eyes when he finally committed to opening them. Then he instinctively pulled his phone, still wired to its charger, off the nightstand. Before he ever saw true daylight, he was staring into his unlit phone screen. For him, nearly every morning began here in this darkness.

Chauncey woke the phone up with his thumb. It was nearly eleven o'clock, too late to surprise his mother and meet her for Sunday service like he'd halfway-hoped to do today. She would have liked that.

This slight disappointment dissipated quickly once he caught sight of the list of notifications waiting for him: an email reminding him that his next credit card payment was soon due, a tag in the drunk pic his friend LeMilion had posted last night, and a club text already advertising tonight's festivities.

And then, there was MENAFTER10. It had missed him while he was sleeping, recovering from his Saturday night out. Six new messages had come in overnight, making his total unread messages 683. Chauncey was all too aware that his flat stomach and fat ass gave him a sort of VIP privilege on the app and that explained his ever-active inbox. Most of the 683 messages he'd accumulated in his years online he mentally discarded upon delivery because they were sent by someone with no pic at all or no pic worthy of his attention.

He tapped the app's neon-colored icon; it was in the shape of the number ten. The number one was a modelesque male silhouette sporting a beard and a backwards-facing basketball cap. The zero was a fat circle with a tight, tiny hole.

The phone filled with the app's background of irradiated blackness. It went with its theme: after hours. MENAFTER10's other colors were various shades of glowing neon. Public pics were bordered in hot pink and a red-light-district-red was outlined around the private ones. Its black and white text alternated inside either dollar bill green or fluorescent violet text bubbles.

With the app open now, Chauncey wasn't Chauncey Lee. Here, he was redNready69, identifiable only by the pics on his profile. Here, he wasn't twenty-four, he was twenty-three. MENAFTER10 didn't require anyone's date of birth so it was up to each user to update their ages after each birthday, manually. Chauncey hadn't gotten around to that just yet, so sure, he was twenty-three. This light-skinned man lying in bed cradling his cell phone matched the rest of the stats listed closely if not exactly. He stopped just the slightest bit short of the five foot six he'd generously given himself and there was a four or five pound difference from the hundred and forty-five pounds he weighed online but he wore these extra pounds well and in a way that didn't really show. As his profile so perfectly put it, Chauncey was a "slim thicc shorty." And slim-thicc was always in on MENAFTER10.

Chauncey didn't bother opening the first of the six waiting messages—redNready69 had a very strict "no pic, no reply" policy.

Hey bro, wanna make some $$$...

It was only spam. So he didn't open the next one either. The third message was legit.

sup

Dry but legit.

Chauncey opened bout2bustb0i's profile, hoping to find something about him to make up for what he lacked in words.

According to his profile, bout2bustb0i was a twenty-eight-year-old, six-foot-tall "masc top down 4 fun." With only a headless torso as his profile pic, Chauncey couldn't argue much against the claim. There wasn't a lot there, but Chauncey extracted enough from what little bout2bustb0i offered about himself to gather some interest. There was something about the scrawniness of his waist that suggested something bigger lay beneath the band of the black boxer-briefs. His imagination filled in what the pic cropped out. And as that picture grew in his head, so did the formation that protruded perpendicularly from his bikini briefs. He saw new potential in the faceless stranger, so much potential that even a simple "sup" seemed charming enough. And even though bout2bustb0i's profile stated "no games or lames allowed," every message, every move, from here on out would be made either to play or get played.

This was MENAFTER10.

bout2bustb0i: *just waking up man. horny af*
redNready69: *same. damn wish i was there*
bout2bustb0i: *unlock?*

On MENAFTER10, unlocking was about the same as undressing. Chauncey, for a moment, hesitated at this request (or was it a command?) to be the first to get naked. Unlike the stranger he was messaging, Chauncey's profile pic featured an actual face, a smooth-skinned, shirtless selfie from the shoulders-up, with a wide smile that showed off white, straight teeth. Even with the silver-studded earrings, two to each ear, and the Roman numerals tattoo of his birthday on his shoulder blade, this picture captured remnants of innocence in the yellow-brown hues of his young face.

The second public pic was less decent and showed Chauncey

in the sterile light of a bathroom holding a phone in front of a mirror in need of cleaning. He wore only gray and blue boxer-briefs, which showed off an ample ass that stretched the limits of the cotton underwear, as well as his six-pack of abs. His rose-colored lips were curved crookedly upwards as he stared at his own reflection, throwing a sly smirk at himself.

Then there were the private pics: the nudes. The first of these had Chauncey stomach down across the same teal sheets he had draped across the bed now but in dimmer lighting. The underexposure of the light combined with the overexposure of the camera's flash was harsh but highlighted his soft and shaven muscly backside. The remaining nudes similarly centered around his ass at different angles and positions, each one more exquisite and explicit than the last.

Chauncey unlocked the profile so that bout2bustb0i could see the private pics and confidently messaged: *you're welcome lol*

Then he waited for the awe, the adulation. He waited a few seconds more for what was sure to be a drool emoji or maybe a wagging tongue. When those didn't appear, he waited longer until a minute had passed, then another minute and then a few more.

Chauncey had sent his wholly nude self out into the infinite digital universe and wondered where had it gone. Had his nakedness gone unnoticed? Was it unseen or unimpressive and unworthy of acknowledgement? As familiar as these questions and their implications were to someone with Chauncey's online experience, they still frightened him. The anxiety he felt as time passed was enough to make him lose his hard-on. He began refreshing the app to update it and show the last time bout-2bustb0i had viewed his now fully open, out-on-the-line profile.

Last viewed: 48 seconds ago.

Chauncey blinked twice.

So that was it, he thought. This was one of those guys that liked to play the pic game. This game was played unfairly by those that tricked private pics out of others under the pretense of a mutual exchange. This was exactly why Chauncey usually enforced a strict "unlock 4 unlock" policy. Just as he thought to relock his profile, a new message came through.

nice

And suddenly everything in the world outside the bedroom, the world he hadn't even walked out into yet, made sense again.

I gotta get in dat yo

With great relief and a wink emoji, Chauncey responded.

and u just might

He hesitated after hitting *Send* because he wasn't sure if this was just a tease or truth.

It didn't matter. Now that he knew he was attractive again, the ball was in his court. He made a request of his own.

unlock yours

For Chauncey, the glowing review his nudes had received counted as the first point in the game between him and bout-2bustb0i. Now that he was in the lead, Chauncey's Sunday morning could start. He set the phone back on the nightstand and got out of the bed begrudgingly. Feeling the beginnings of a mild hangover, he gave his body a few seconds to balance itself before putting it into motion by opening the vinyl window blinds and inviting the harsh sunlight into his bedroom.

It took a moment for his eyes to adjust before he could notice how the light hit the steel bones of the building-to-be across the street. Chauncey didn't know what they were building exactly, probably more of those fancy condos that were taking over this part of town, but whatever it was, it was a disturbance to him in both sight and sound. Today, however, there was a way in which the sun shone through the battered blue tarp that hung over the metal and wood frame that made it less bothersome to look at. If this bright new day could do that to the building, Chauncey was excited about what it could do for him.

Even if he had woken up too late to make it to Sunday service on time, maybe it was worth going anyway, if only to see his mother's face decide on if she was happy to see him or mad he'd shown up so goddamn late. He wouldn't care which one it was. It would just be nice to see her. Maybe he could go back home with her and help her cook dinner while his weeks' worth of laundry was in the washer. Might even hit up the gym after, stop and pick up some wine on his way home so he could get back and relax and fall asleep to an episode of *Victims: NYC*.

Yes, *this* was the day Chauncey wanted for himself, he decided as he stared out of his limited fourth-story view of the latest change to the neighborhood. But before he could step out into what was sure to be a beautiful day just beyond what the construction obscured, he had to wash off all of last night.

The unusual silence outside of Chauncey's bedroom meant that neither of his two roommates were home. He quickly seized this opportunity to claim the bathroom while it was free. He ran himself a hot shower, taking his time to rinse off Saturday night. There had been the drinks, so many and so cheap, that were responsible for the faint redness in his eyes right now, so he let the water spray his face. Then there was the sweat in his pores from the dry sex he called dancing, so he made sure to scrub his cracks and crevices thoroughly. His hair had soaked up smoke from the dark corners and seedier sections of the club, so he made a point to scratch shampoo deep into his scalp. And that night and its worldliness, no matter how recent it was, went down the shower drain with the last suds of soap that splashed off of him. He emerged from the bathroom fragrant with the scent of artificial coconut and returned to his bedroom just in time to catch his phone sound. It wasn't a bell. It wasn't a chirp. This warped tone was specific to MENAFTER10.

10

The game Chauncey had already forgotten he was playing resumed. There was a new notification.

PROFILE UNLOCKED: bout2bustb0i

He didn't hesitate to explore what he was now privy to. He tapped the screen, his finger still slightly wet, and the phone lit up, as did his face. As he held the phone closer looking at the picture, the towel wrapped around his waist became undone and Chauncey's arousal returned, pointing itself upwards at the uncoiled delight on the display in an extreme close-up. The phone was filled with so much brown—thick, lumpy, day-old-gravy-brown—that it almost stretched from one corner to the next uninterrupted by any other color. It looked as nasty as Chauncey wanted it to be when he imagined it being plunged inside him and being used like the tool it was. The dick was so big it could hardly fit on the screen, no matter which way he turned it; it would certainly never fit in with church or dinner with Mama or the gym or *Victims: NYC* or any of the rest of the day Chauncey wished he wanted for himself more than he wanted to get fucked right now.

The round mounds of ass Chauncey Lee was carrying bulged out of his baggy red basketball shorts like two big bubbles of flesh and fabric. A small, plain, white T-shirt underneath a thin gray hoodie did little to conceal what the low-hanging shorts failed to. Chauncey's toned calves looked especially muscular in this sporty get-up and his multicolored sneakers and lack of visible socks highlighted them even more. By the time he'd made a left on Katherine Avenue, Chauncey had racked up more than a few lustful eyes in his trek from the train station to Katherine Square, eyes whose heat pierced through the flimsy fabric of his red shorts.

Chauncey had noticed the stares; they flattered him. The

adulation may have been silent on the subway and street but he heard it in his swelling head louder than he heard the music that was beating into his ears from his earbuds. With all this noise in his head, he was at a disadvantage, being unable to hear the painful past of Katherine Square that screamed out from the stains on the very concrete he was walking on as he approached it.

Katherine Square, the two blocks of small businesses and residences between Christian Memorial Hospital and Court Street, had always had a history with men like Chauncey. How that history came to be, no one could remember exactly. What everyone could remember was the public hospital on Christian Avenue and the adjacent tower of apartments over on Katherine Avenue, which had at one point been public housing units.

Decades earlier, long before Chauncey was born, one of the men of "the lifestyle" who lived in the apartment tower had fallen ill with an ailment that no one had a name for at the time. He died. Then another did the same. Then another. And then more, many more. Most of the men who died were unmarried and unassociated with any woman that anyone knew of anyway. Not only that but they all seemed to be familiar with one another. They had all been seen visiting that unusual men's bar just down the street. Some of them even lived together as roommates or friends. Afraid of what was happening to the neighborhood, more and more residents of Katherine Square gathered the spit to call them out for what they suspected they were—faggots, queers, punks, abominations all too deserving of the disease that would go on to be called AIDS.

AIDS hit the neighborhood in a very specific way, sickening the men in and around the Katherine Square apartments until they were taken into the hospital across the street to likely die. Some folks called the two buildings—the apartment tower and the hospital—"the gloom and doom twins." In time, because most of the ill and uninsured who died were, initially at least, men from "that queer street," no one wanted to live on it and so a certain reputation cemented itself between Katherine

Square's dingy bricks.

Now here was Chauncey Lee walking through this history, their history, with his ass exposed to the spirits of men just like him who had already been where he was only just going. He walked without the slightest caution, mumbling the words to music put together with such minimum effort its lyrics read like the caption of the last pic he'd posted to social media. He didn't even look up at the ancient apartment building he was approaching with its worn, woeful ten floors, covered with unwashed brick and mostly untouched by recent renovation. The large, engulfing backdrop of Christian Memorial Hospital stood several stories above it. At this very moment, the hospital was backlit by the sun so the building's shadow swept over the apartments almost entirely.

The coolness of the sudden shade against Chauncey's skin stole his attention from the thumping bass of the music to the building, now known as The Katherine Square Residences, according to the sign posted at the entrance. The discoloration in the white plastic lettering was ominous enough to make him stop to double-check the address bout2bustb0i had sent. Sighing, he approached the mouth of the building, which was guarded by a gate and a call box. Chauncey popped out his ear pods and texted into his phone: *code?*

He hit *Send* and stood waiting in the unfamiliar neighborhood, hands idle, the small glee he'd felt earlier slowly seeping out of him. The unfriendly atmosphere of the street tightened his expression and straightened his back. He felt uncomfortable being here and even more uncomfortable being here alone. The sight of an older Black woman dressed in her crisp and colorful Sunday's best holding her grandson by the hand, one hand small and smooth and one hand wrinkled and touched by time, helped put him at ease. It was a delight to see, at first. Then it was something else. Chauncey wasn't sure what exactly, but it made him think of his mother and why he wasn't with her right now, walking her home from church.

Was it too late for that? he wondered.

13

Everything had happened so fast since bout2bustb0i's first text. Sure, he could have tried putting off meeting up with him until later that day but MENAFTER10 promoted a certain urgency. Almost everyone who was looking was looking for now and anything later than now often led to never. So Chauncey took this feeling that was tugging at him and charged it to the game and the rapid speed at which it was played.

His phone buzzed.

bout2bustb0i: *call 7891*

Chauncey dialed the number on the call box just as the neat little grandmother and grandson made their way past him. There was a purity in them that seemed to freshen up the whole neighborhood for a second. The love between them that Chauncey inhaled as they passed smelled like the sweet breath of a baby after being fed warm milk.

"Hey," Chauncey said, somewhere in the general direction of the grandmother and grandson. The tot-sized boy caught his wayward greeting eagerly and returned it with a loud "Hey!" shot back at Chauncey with unrestrained friendliness. Chauncey watched the little boy and his little grandmother as they continued further down the street, further from him and all his about-to-get-fuckedness.

"Hello," said the mumbled baritone coming from the call box.

The blunt force of its tone startled the smile off of Chauncey's face. Then, remembering the game he was in, he leaned into the call box, speaking into it in his best baritone.

"Aye, it's me," he said in a fast, faux, and foreign voice, so different from the light airiness he'd used with the grandmother and grandson that was his normal speaking voice. He sounded silly, even to himself, and not just because of the fake voice he was using.

"It's me." *Me* could have been anyone. *Me* could have been Santa Claus's churchgoing cousin or the man on the moon.

14

Chauncey wished he had said his name instead, even if the man on the call box wouldn't know who that was either.

The call box didn't care. It emitted a high-pitched chime and let in the unknown man in red shorts and directed him downstairs.

The basement level of the Katherine Square Residences betrayed the beautiful Sunday that lay above it. The corridor floor was dusty and scuffed. With no windows, there was no sun. The only lighting was provided by mismatched strips of fluorescent lights along the low ceiling, each one a slightly different wattage than the next, creating a dim, menacing ambience. A damp smell hung in the air and made Chauncey walk carefully so he wouldn't brush against the walls that might be touched with mildew.

After ringing the doorbell to apartment 1114, Chauncey began to mentally calculate how much rent the property management must knock off for living down on this level. The door was unlocked before he could finish the mathematics and a six-foot-tall stranger in sweat shorts opened it.

"Aye. Wassup. You can come in," he said in a quick mumble. His masculinity was just as believable in person as it was online. Chauncey liked that.

"Wassup," Chauncey replied in a forced monotone. He stepped into the apartment which was lit only by what sunlight came through its two small windows. He was somewhat surprised to find the one-bedroom looked so lived-in, like it was home to more life than just a bachelor renter. He counted at least five framed pictures placed around the living room and there was what looked to be a child's messy, stick-figured drawing clipped to the refrigerator. Maybe it was from a niece or nephew, he thought. The aroma of a recently cooked breakfast hung in the air. Pan sausage. Chauncey couldn't quite make out what had been cooked to accompany it. Scrambled eggs, perhaps?

"You can sit down," said bout2bustb0i, gesturing towards the earth-tone sofa. The sofa, like the rest of the furniture, was built for a house, not a small apartment, and took up too much space. Chauncey discovered that with the soft and cushioning nature of the sofa, one didn't so much sit down—they sank down.

bout2bustb0i shut the door and locked it—bolt, latch and knob. His face was a dull, unmoisturized brown and looked even more ordinary than Chauncey remembered from the one pic that featured it on his MENAFTER10 profile. So, instead, Chauncey looked at the bulge in his cotton shorts. There, right there, bunched up, was bout2bustb0i's redeeming quality.

bout2bustb0i caught Chauncey gaping at him. Chauncey tried to turn his head, but it was too late. Chauncey knew he'd seen him because he was grinning when he sat and joined him in the pit of the sofa. Sitting pushed up bout2bustb0i's shorts and made the outline of peen so prominent Chauncey could almost trace its veins. He forced himself to look away before he got lost between the long, skinny legs and turned his attention to the TV instead.

"What were you thinking . . . out there on that stage?" asked the shapely Black woman on the TV screen.

Chauncey was happy to see her heavily made-up face. *The Mary Divine Show* was a favorite of his. He recognized today's episode from the highlights and memes on his timeline. Everyone was talking about it—Mary Divine's interview with Aura Era mere days after she performed live on *Martin in tha Morning* and flubbed her performance. She blamed it on the sound engineers, dubbing it a "technological misunderstanding." The gossip blogs blamed it on all her incessant partying post-breakup with actor Luke Chevy and were calling for her head. With her colorful delivery of questions that lay somewhere between serious and satirical, Mary Divine was intent on serving it to them. Aura was doing her best to sell herself as a pretty little ponytailed victim as she answered each question with the delicacy of a kitten.

"What is going on? Why is this happening to me? I was mortified. Absolutely mortified," she said softly, holding back tears that never seemed to come. "In that moment, *that* was all I could think."

"Was *that* all you could sing too?" Mary quipped back.

This was Chauncey's favorite part of what he'd seen of the interview. He wanted to say *KO! Victory! C'mon, Mary Divine with the finish! Fatality bitch! Yasss!* But he gagged the queen trying to pry open the corners of his mouth.

"Shit. That bitch a savage," bout2bustb0i said over an unbridled bark of laughter, the kind Chauncey wished he had, deep and masculine.

Chauncey took this as permission to let out a hushed giggle in place of the explosion of elation he was holding in.

"My bad. You wanna watch something? I can change it," bout2bustb0i offered.

"Oh no. I'm good," Chauncey replied with as much make-pretend bass as he could muster.

bout2bustb0i changed the channel anyway, combing through cartoons, commercials, and several reality shows before finally settling on *Coming Back to Creation*. Chauncey wished he hadn't. *Coming Back to Creation* was a movie, and movies came with strings. In Chauncey's mind, it was pointless to get invested in something that required a ninety-minute-to-two-hour commitment knowing that neither of them had any intention of finishing it. At some point, one of them would have to interrupt it to incite the action they intended to have. Chauncey thought it was harder to tell the appropriate time to do so with a movie. He had already seen *Coming Back to Creation* and "wanna fuck?" would seem out of place so soon after Luna lost husband number three, he thought.

They were both ready for sex now actually, but since they didn't know each other, they didn't know how to tell the other. So they misread uncertainty as shyness and sat in silence watching Luna Duval cry her heart out. After waiting impatiently for grief to transform the talented chanteuse into a chain-smoking recluse, Chauncey found a slightly more appropriate opportunity to ask. "So, you trynna do somethin' or nah?"

"Shit yeah," bout2bustb0i quickly answered, his eyes shimmering with lust.

They could act honestly now. Chauncey exhaled, no longer bothering to use his butch voice and bout2bustb0i dropped the pretense of politeness, instead sliding his sweats down over his legs.

Chauncey closed the gap between them, shifted himself on the sofa, put his hand into bout2bustb0i's cheap blue boxer-briefs and pulled out a droopy black dick. He held it fondly, slowly massaging it to life. It took only seconds for it to become firm and turn into a hard slab of flesh. Seeing in person what he'd only seen in pics, Chauncey's own aroused dick stabbed against the lining of his shorts. He removed them, as well as his socks, shoes and jacket, and kneeled before bout2bustb0i's throbbing enlargement.

"Take off yo' shirt," bout2bustb0i commanded.

Chauncey's T-shirt came off, revealing his nakedness. He parted his pink lips and, eyes shut, softly threw his head into the stranger's erection. His mouth engulfed it in one smooth, delicate sweep. The radiating heat of its firmness hit the roof of his mouth. As it filled the whole of Chauncey's mouth, tickling it with its strong veins, a drop of the salty, sloppy wetness spilled out and splattered into the sofa cushion.

Chauncey continued to feed on it until he was stopped.

"Let's go in the room," bout2bustb0i muttered, almost unable to form the words.

Chauncey sucked the stem in one last, long, drool-laden draw before releasing it. When he opened his eyes and looked up, bout2bustb0i was looking down at him, proudly, petting the top of his head as he knelt before him, doe-eyed, eager and dribbling at the mouth.

"You like dat, huh?" he said as if speaking to a dog that had just been given a treat.

Chauncey's two ruby pillows of lips, greased and creased,

turned up in a devilish direction to form a smirk. It was a smirk that deserved disrespect, that wanted it, so bout2bustb0i slapped it with his wet dick. The smirk stayed. bout2bustb0i's eyes wondered what else that smirk wanted him to do. He got up off the couch, kicked off his sweat shorts, and led Chauncey to the bedroom with his stiff nakedness swinging in the stale air of the apartment.

Once they made it in the room, bout2bustb0i got to removing his remaining articles of clothing, taking off his T-shirt and socks. There was a warmth here in the bedroom that Chauncey could feel the moment his first bare foot stepped into it and out of the shadows that covered everywhere else in the amber-lit apartment. Chauncey certainly didn't claim to be the most observant person, but he could have sworn the sun wasn't where it should have been, considering he'd been walking towards it when he was going down Katherine Avenue a short while ago. Being that he was now at the base of the building and he believed the apartment faced Court Street, which was completely opposite Christian Memorial Hospital (the direction he remembered the sunlight coming in from), Chauncey couldn't quite figure out how it was possible for the sun to shift itself and shine so abundantly here. Not only that, but he questioned how it could come down at such a direct angle through the small, single window stuck at the very top of the wall with a gutter-level view of the street. But then again, maybe he'd just had it all wrong.

bout2bustb0i's two big hands latched onto Chauncey's tight waist from behind and applied soft pressure. Chauncey took the hint and climbed atop the messy bed, knees-first. He posed at the edge of the bed, head facing down, behind lifted high. bout-2bustb0i admired his form before taking his hand and letting two fingers slip into the crack of Chauncey's backside, pleased to find slight moisture. He coated his fingertips in the dew and sniffed them: they smelled of a mild mustiness. Sourishly sweet, slightly sweaty, the scent aroused him all the more and he led himself into Chauncey.

"You got a rubber?" Chauncey asked quickly. He was proud

of himself for asking; it was a rare attempt at growth. There had once been a time when he'd thought of himself as forever young and therefore immune to everything from contracting HIV to getting into a car crash. But then there had been syphilis. And gonorrhea. He had every intention of one day making full use of his mediocre health insurance with regular doctor's visits and getting a prescription for PreX, that HIV-prevention medication he was always seeing commercials about, but that day simply wasn't today.

"Oh, shit. Yeah," bout2bustb0i apologized, but there was no sincerity in his voice. There was annoyance.

Chauncey lay still on the messy bed as bout2bustb0i walked over and reached into the top drawer of the nightstand and removed a condom. The familiar sounds of the wrapper being unpeeled and the latex being suited was a comfort for Chauncey but also slightly disappointing. He hadn't wanted to make this request any more than bout2bustb0i had wanted to honor it. But, growth.

bout2bust0b0i climbed onto the bed and slipped his sheathed self into Chauncey, carefully easing in before his pokes turned into purpose-driven pushes. Chauncey contained his discomfort as quietly as he could, but as the pain persisted, he began to writhe.

"You don't got no lube?" he asked in frustration.

The pain came to a sudden stop. Even from behind, Chauncey could sense the bewilderment on bout2bustb0i's face. Maybe he had thought the lump of spit he'd let fall out of his mouth and onto his dick had been enough. Nonetheless, he reached his long arm all the way over to the nightstand and rummaged the top drawer without removing himself from inside Chauncey.

"Shit. Not really. I mean, I got something . . ." he trailed off. "It ain't no lube, though."

Chauncey dislodged the dick out of him and turned around. A small, used bottle of off-brand shea butter was pointed at him, its grimy price tag nearly peeled off.

"Shea butter?" Chauncey asked flatly. "That's all you got?"

"Yeah, dis' pretty much it," bout2bustb0i replied matter-of-factly.

Chauncey quickly considered solutions to this unexpected problem. "Damn. Ain't no store close by or nothin'?"

"Yeah. The corner store right up there. Ain't you pass it?" bout2bustb0i said without so much as blinking.

It was a valid point. Chauncey had passed by the store. He had also assumed that his host would have lube. He was beginning to feel stupid for expecting that much of him.

He'd been in pinches like this before but he had never succumbed to shea butter up the butt from a stranger. Maybe it wouldn't be so bad. He could just go along with it this time and throw growth out the gutter-level window . . . but shea butter? What was next? Shampoo? Olive oil? Acne cream? Where exactly did he draw the line when it came to what he would and would not allow? Was there a line? And what about the condom? What would the shea butter do to it? he wondered. Maybe he should just walk down to the corner store, ask the Korean cashier for the least expensive bottle of lube from behind the counter, and come back. If only he wasn't feeling so lazy at this very moment. Maybe they could just jerk off instead and he could get what he came there for, albeit in a less-enjoyable way, put the red shorts back on and go home and take his second shower of the day. He began to long for that second shower. The day had dirtied him enough already.

bout2bustb0i broke this train of thought when he began messily rubbing the shea butter onto the rubber condom. It didn't look right—heaps of butter on black latex, mixed with a little saliva and bodily secretion. It looked like a homemade project gone wrong, like some kind of do-it-yourself dick. Then he massaged some of the pale-colored shea butter into Chauncey. It was cool and creamy and kind of tickled. Chauncey slowly began to warm up to the idea of shea butter. After the yellowish ooze had been unevenly applied, Chauncey felt comfortable enough to reposition himself into a more accommodating angle, bringing his ass back and his head down. bout2bustb0i appreciated this act of cooperation and thanked him for it by ramming himself into Chauncey from behind, repeatedly.

The soft stream of sunlight grazed Chauncey's spine. He looked up at the awkwardly placed window where all the light in the world, it seemed, was pouring through the blinds. He could see how he must have looked right now from that point of view, getting smutted out on a Sunday. He might have looked bad from that angle but it was all a matter of lighting, really. What he was doing right now would have looked different had it been night. The night and its shadows would have been much more forgiving and wouldn't have shown every little detail, his every little fuck-up, so clearly. It wouldn't show him in this light. That's what he liked about night. He wished it would come soon.

Maybe, he hoped, under this most intimate ray of the sun, there was some small speck of redemption for him somewhere floating in the dust. But with the funk of sex in the air and sweat on his face and friction-heated shea butter seeping into him, he didn't look too hard for it. Besides, by the time night fell, he would be gone and so would the day that could have been.

CHAPTER 2

HAT MAN

"Oh, dat bitch bad."

Lust crusted over his lips as he spoke.

Justin noticed this because unlike the other men occupying the Uncommon Kutz barbershop, his eyes weren't on the image of the beauty queen on the TV screen. They were on the barber who was commentating on the program.

"What country dat hoe from?" he went on. "Colombia? Shit, Colombia got all da pretty hoes, huh? Shit, I might have to gimme a passport. Ya know, I ain't neva had no Colombia pussy. Look at her. Look at dem nice-ass titties. She don't got no ass, doe. All she gotta do is get some ass and dat's it. Still fuck her, doe."

There were three barbers on duty, but the Colombian Pussy-Wanter was the loudest. Justin was keeping his eyes on him in particular because, as a first-time visitor and walk-in, he was subject to be cut by the first barber who had an open chair. And since Pussy-Wanter was clearly a talker, the more the TV distracted him and the more he talked his shit, the more time it would take for him to finish with the tall teenage boy who looked like he played varsity basketball, Justin hoped. It had taken a lot for Justin to come here. With his undiagnosed and untreated depression the way that it was, it took a lot to go anywhere these days—to work, to the grocery store, hell, to the mailbox. There were some days he couldn't even make it to the bathroom to brush his teeth or wash his ass.

So even Justin was surprised he was here, after a day of work no less. It was nice to know he still had enough strength to drag himself into the first barbershop he could find, just before it closed, to wander in wearing those tight jeans and ask, "Can anybody cut me?" in his feminine voice to a room of unfriendly faces.

Pussy-Wanter had taken his time before responding with a cold and ambiguous "Bet," Justin recalled, thinking of all the many reasons he didn't want the delicate matter that was his hair to be cared for by a *dusty, low-to-the-ground lil' nigga* who was too insecure to even look him in the eyes just because he was clearly uncomfortable around the blatantly gay customers that visited the shop.

But as luck would have it, Pussy-Wanter was the first of the three to finish and have a free chair. Justin saw from the razor-sharp lineup and smooth fade etched into the head he'd just finished that the little fucker wasn't without skill. Might not be so bad.

The Pussy-Wanter dusted off the chair and shifted his eyes in Justin's direction without making eye contact and risking any chance of contracting gayness. Justin realized this was his way of calling him to come, so he stood up in his skinny jeans and approached the chair, closing the gap between him and the Pussy-Wanter. The busted leather chair was freshly warmed from the last customer. Though left behind by a stranger, it was a friendly heat and Justin didn't mind the way it hit the back of his thighs.

Pussy-Wanter tied the thin cape to the new customer in the chair. Justin could smell the begrudgement lotioned into his hands as he tied the knot loosely, lazily but careful to make as minimal physical contact as possible.

"You gon' take off yo' cap, bruh?" he asked in a voice distinctly different from his Miss Colombia commentary, distinctly dry.

Somehow, Justin had forgotten about the black baseball cap

over his head and that getting a haircut required its removal. There were restaurants and clubs with "no hats allowed" policies that he didn't go to anymore because he didn't go anywhere without one. Hats had become his best friend in the months since he'd last paid a visit to the barber. His hesitation in having to part with such a close friend began to tighten the cape around his neck and restrict his intake of the air that fumed with alcohol and gentlemanly aftershave.

All at once, Justin sprung up out of the chair and stood on his feet.

Everyone was staring at him, prepared to defend themselves at any moment against this sudden movement that had made them all dangerously uncomfortable.

Reminding himself of what part of town he was in, he pitched his voice especially low as he explained, "I'mma just wait."

"Wait? Fa' what?" Pussy-Wanter asked, stumped, startled, steamed.

"I'mma wait on him," Justin said, pointing his eyes farther down the hallway-sized barbershop and praying they'd land somewhere that made sense.

The room's attention all panned to the back where the quieter barber was, the third one, who had been minding his business the whole time.

"Duke?" Pussy-Wanter asked, just as confused as everyone else.

"I can cut him," Duke said, quickly, covering his surprise. Justin's head had belonged to Pussy-Wanter the moment he had sat down in his chair. Heads didn't have the right to hop chairs and they both knew that. He took a proper look at Justin and his demeanor, instantly aware of his lone, open gayness in the shop and, understanding the situation, casually added, "I got him."

He was breaking a rule. They both were.

Justin set his sights on his co-conspirator. Duke was built softly, his cheeks were full, and there was just the right amount of pudginess around his waist. The meat on his bones made him

25

look more like a lightweight teddy bear than a full-on tank, though. Seeing the way the whites of his eyes were shining even from this distance, Justin felt Duke's face was a place he could rest his reservations.

He exhaled on instinct.

"Then why da fuck you sat down den?" Pussy-Wanter spat out at him.

Just for that, Justin chose to fling the weightless cape back into the chair.

He could hear him mumbling something hostile, something involving "fucking faggots," as he walked to the back of the shop. Justin told himself he didn't quite hear what was said. He didn't have the energy to hear it, to respond to it, to defend himself against it, to do anything other than get this damn haircut, and he hardly had it in him to do that.

Duke greeted him, "Just lemme finish up and you next, man."

Justin nodded in acknowledgment and sat and waited until the last chunk of coiled hair from the head before him had fallen to the floor.

Duke motioned for him, letting him know that he was ready.

"How ya doin', man?" asked Duke as he went in for a hand-shake.

"Hey. What's up?" Justin replied as he got a touch of the moisturized tenderness of the hand in his hand.

"You can sit down. I'll be right back. Just gotta take a quick piss."

Justin was already so sold on Duke's saintliness from their brief interaction that even a word like *piss* sounded polite on him.

There was no edge to his voice, Justin noted as he made himself comfortable in the chair and ignored the occasional stare from the disgruntled Pussy-Wanter. Unlike him, Duke's voice was clear and chipper. So many of the straights these days talked like they were gargling gravel, Justin thought. Not Duke. His voice wasn't like that. It didn't huff or puff. It was relaxed, hardened by absolutely nothing. Other descriptions came to his mind as he sat idly in the chair. His attention eventually turned to the mirror on the wall and the man it showed him, the man with the hat stuck to this head, the man who looked lost, the man who *was* lost, the man with a fatter face than he had had a few months ago.

Those eyebrows, though. They were lights on a dim face.

So much had gone to hell in the recent months—his physique, his self-esteem. Even still, he had somehow managed his eyebrows' upkeep when he wasn't managing much else. They had remained strong, wide and full through it all.

Justin had always had a good pair of brows, though.

"Eyebrows are the anchor to the face, honey," he had been quoted as saying to the many people he encountered who had taken the time out to appreciate the two arches above his eyes.

He said it to himself as he looked in the mirror and remembered that he at least had one thing left that was physically redeemable. Maybe, he thought, that was all he needed to make up for the rest.

"Alright, my man," Duke interrupted. "What's going on witchu tonight?"

"Huh?" Justin responded with uncertain defensiveness, the result of the social rustiness he'd accumulated lately.

Duke didn't flinch. "What you doin' tonight, man?"

There was an obvious innocence behind the question, but Justin was exhausted thinking of all the things it demanded from him these days. He didn't know what he was doing tonight, nor did he know what he would like to be doing tonight. Used to be that he loved going out for dinner with friends and trying new restaurants and dishes he'd never heard of, but this bout of depression had changed that. He didn't have the energy to go out. If he got hungry now, he ate at home.

The truth was that this Saturday night was likely to be as uneventful as last Saturday night and even the Saturday night before that one. This hadn't always been the case. It was just lately and Justin liked to think of lately as just a rut he was stuck in, one that he would one day get out of, no matter how hard it was to see that day through the depths of his despondency.

Lately, Justin didn't love anything. Lately, it was too expensive to go out to the places he was invited to, places that were probably too crowded or too loud or didn't allow hats. He was getting too old to be staying out too late anyway, too tired from work, too blah to be partying, or sometimes, he thought, he was just too ugly.

And lately, with all the things going on in the news, staying in was safer than going out, he told himself sometimes. He could be actually dead at twenty-nine rather than just socially dead, although there were times when he wished for the former. Anything to put an end to the nagging nothingness inside him.

Once upon a time, he had been fun, though. Once upon a time, he had been one of the cute, skinny queens on the scene.

It was better to leave the streets with memories of that person than this one.

And so rested the social life of Justin Berry.

That was the truth but Duke was a stranger. In the presence of a stranger, he could be whoever he wanted. He could be someone with a life.

"Um, nothing much really. Might run through Elysian Row and see what's happening," he lied.

"Elysian Row? Whew," said Duke. "I ain't been out there on a Saturday night in a minute."

Justin restrained himself from lying again. As Duke tied the cape around his neck, Justin caught a whiff of his scent. It was mostly aftershave and the alcohol-based products he worked with all day, sweet and acidic, but there was a hint of something else. It could have been as simple as his deodorant but whatever it was, the smell was cool and clean. Although Justin got only a sniff of it, it seemed like a friendly smell to him that made him think of the color blue.

Duke adjusted the chair, sinking Justin just beneath his chest.

"Take off ya hat for me, man."

28

Justin gulped, swallowing his reluctance.

The jig was up. Every day of the last few months he'd let gone to waste was about to be revealed, along with every trip to the gym he hadn't taken, every friend he'd turned into a stranger, every part of him that he'd let go into neglect.

Finally, he surrendered and did what was asked of him, uncovering the matted thatch of hair from underneath the cap.

Justin's eyes turned back to the mirror. He had deliberately not spent much time looking in mirrors as of late and when he did, he was usually wearing a hat. He couldn't recall the last time he'd seen himself without one. Since he was a child, Justin had always been told that his wavy, jet-black curls were "good hair." Now, most of his "good hair" was still there but under the off-white light in the shop, there was noticeable recession at the front.

There was also The Spot.

The Spot was his private name for the patch on the crown of his head where his hair thinned, his baldness became visible, and he became fucking ugly.

In the span of the two years since he'd first discovered it, it'd gone from what he deemed a small, quarter-sized problem area into what it was today: a gash through which what was left of his once luscious ringlets of hair, once active sex life, once healthy confidence, once happier self, all bled out.

The hat sealed that hole.

It didn't feel right holding it in his lap, Justin thought. It should be on his head. But getting a whiff of the hat's odor from too much wear and not enough washing, Justin resisted the urge to put it back on his head.

He sat there in the chair, waiting for whatever came next, anxious and unsure of what this man was about to do to him. All that would come next, though, was Duke's pick, softly digging into Justin's head. Justin could feel the change in pace once he reached The Spot and the hair pick struggled to catch quite as many strands to rake out.

"Alright. What we gettin'?" Duke asked, upbeat and clearly

accustomed to seeing Spots just like Justin's.

Justin's last trip to the barbershop had been his last trip to the barbershop because of this very question.

"Bald fade," he had said that last time. This was somewhat of a constant hairstyle for Justin. It was clean and safe—two things he tried to be, in his own way.

"Okay. I got you. I might have to cut it a little lower to even you out, though," the last barber had warned. "It's gettin' a lil' thin right here."

Justin didn't like his hair with all the fun cut out of it. Neither did anyone else, it seemed to him. By his count, the lower his fades got, the fewer DMs he got, the fewer likes he got, the fewer men he could get. It was hard to tell what was and wasn't hyperbole because it was around the same time as his last haircut that the depression returned with its feet planted on Justin's neck.

It had come and created a new image of himself, adding up the nearly thirty years he'd spent surviving as a Black, gay man and multiplying them. It made sure he was aware that he was now going to need to find something besides pretty hair to survive being Black and gay in the world. It wasn't enough that he worked and had his own apartment. If he was going to be Black, he was going to need a donkey dick. If he was going to be gay, he was going to need the ass or abs of Adonis. If he was going to be Black *and* gay, he was going to need them all. He'd been getting by for far too long with his "good" hair and now that he didn't have that anymore, he was purely mediocre.

Until he found the necessary money or popularity to compensate for this, Justin figured he could save himself the thirty bucks he was spending every two weeks and cut his own hair. So he bought some clippers and taught himself how to do something even simpler, a buzzcut. He wasn't very good at it but as far as grooming went, he got the job done. And he was saving money. But The Spot was still there. The buzzcuts he was giving himself only dulled it, made it less apparent.

He needed it gone for good.

If he was already a fine hair away from being bald, he reck-oned, maybe he'd be better off being bald. There could be no Spot if there was no hair.

There were men that pulled it off, even some his age. Maybe he could be one of those men, one of the ones that made bald-ness look fashionable, look sexy even.

So, one night he mustered up the courage to do it, to make bald the new him. He picked up the clippers and cut through the center of his head. Then, he took his disposable razor and shaved it down until there was nothing but skin that was sleek, shiny and Spot-free. He put his hands on this skin that hadn't been seen before and brushed his fingers on its slick and unfa-miliar surface. He had looked at this bold, new effort of his in the mirror with a hard and heavy glare and all he could see was his father.

Justin had always hated that he looked so much like his father, having inherited his same wide nose, same big lips. Joseph Berry had always been bald, from Justin's first memory of him to his last. He had wondered what his father looked like now, since that last time.

No use of thinking of a nigga that ain't thinking of you, he had told himself as he scrolled through his limited selection of memories of the man who hadn't told him this day would come so soon. The man that had never even been around to teach him how to pick up a razor. The man who was the reason why he never learned how to pick up himself.

Justin grew his hair back and told himself he would do whatever was left for him to do to look as little like that excuse for a man as possible, turning next to vitamins and eating more vegetables, then oils and ointments.

And until they kicked in, hats every day.

He learned to put a hat over his problems and go to work and pay his bills and eat and cook and function just enough for no one to see what was going on underneath it all.

Until today.

"Oh my God. I forgot you had hair underneath that," Marie

from work, bless her heart, had said just earlier today, an innocent observation of the overgrown hair protruding out from underneath the baseball cap.

But Justin had heard her differently.

Underneath *that*.

That was what had brought him into the closest barbershop he could find. *That* guy who wears the hats every fucking day. *That* hat man. *That* freak. How had he let things get *that* bad? He didn't care what Duke did to his hair. He just didn't want to be *that*.

But Justin didn't know how to articulate this to a stranger, so all he could say was, "Um" when Duke asked him what he wanted done.

Duke was patient and tried feeding him some suggestions.

"You wanna keep the top or you wanna just half it? Or you wanna just go even all around?"

"Um, yeah," Justin said, his voice so low even he wasn't sure words had come out. "Kinda."

"Kinda what, though?" Duke persisted.

"Kinda . . . whatever," Justin answered with his head down.

Duke paused, hearing the way the words fell out of Justin's mouth and realizing there was a person sitting in his chair who needed more than a haircut. He needed a hug, a night of drunken laughter between friends, maybe even therapy. It had been a long day for Duke. He'd counted each head he'd cut today and calculated what it could pay towards his booth rental or his boys' back-to-school supplies.

This last head of the night would do little to pay any of those looming costs but it would afford him a reminder of what made the still new and unfamiliar experience of working in this poorly managed head shop in the hood worth it all.

Duke knew exactly what to do.

"Alright. I'mma get you right, my man."

This assurance relaxed Justin almost as much as the weight of the hand resting on his tense shoulder did. The quiet buzz of the clippers rolling against his scalp only brought on more comfort, comfort that eventually gathered in the corners of his eyelids and closed them. He could rest his worries. His head was in good hands.

With Duke's help, Justin's hairline had become a bed of pure, uninterrupted blackness. The sides were faded with two parts cut into his left temple. The top was low but high enough to be brushed and show some texture, and every angle was lined with straight-edged precision.

Besides the thirty dollars and ten dollar tip, this transformation came with one other cost.

"I got you right, my man. I filled in the top so I could get it nice and even. If you don't wash it out or nothin', it should last a few days. A week, tops." Duke was still holding the small bottle of Redoo, semi-permanent hair dye and darkening solution.

Looking at the image of this full-haired man in the mirror distracted Justin from this disclaimer. He was willing to do whatever was required to look like this as often as possible, even if it meant spending thirty dollars every week to piece and paint this exquisiteness back on.

"Got it," Justin acknowledged.

"Alright, man. Enjoy your night," Duke wished his last cut for the night good-bye.

They shook hands in farewell and Justin made sure to squeeze as much gratitude as he could into Duke's hand—for the healing power of a haircut, for the stories about his two kids and "not so bad" babies' mama.

"Thanks, man. You too."

Justin turned around in the direction of the door. He wasn't sure if it was him or his new hair that told him to Naomi Campbell-walk his way past the Pussy-Wanter and cut his eyes at him as he said "g'night" in his gayest voice. He pushed the door open and flipped his hair, both the filled-in and the entirely fictional, before leaving the puzzled pussy-wanters staring behind as he strutted off into the night.

Justin felt he looked too good to go home so he followed through on what he had said earlier and took the subway to Elysian Row, a small commercial district of mostly Black-owned bars and restaurants. He didn't plan to stay long. He was just there to show off the greatness that had been put atop his head to the waves of not-yet-drunk young people out on the strip early.

He stumbled into some good lighting under a marquee and decided to snap a pic of the marvelous thing Duke had made of him. Looking down into the cracked phone screen at the image of the new him and the way the flash lit him around the eyes just right, drawing attention to the loyal pair of anchors that had always held him together, he would deem it profile pic material.

It would be the first pic he had posted to social media in a very long time.

People were already "liking" it, people he hadn't seen or spoken to in ages. Why had it been so long again? he wondered, his memory skipping over the ignored texts, unreturned phone calls or declined invitations that were responsible.

None of that mattered now, so he texted his old roommate Trina. He DM'd his friend De'Leon.

Then someone brushed his shoulder. It was a passerby in locs and a loose, oversized T-shirt that criminally covered the hard body Justin had felt so briefly. He didn't look back. He just walked straight ahead, not noticing the new potential painted on Justin's head.

It deserved to be seen, by this random fine-ass and maybe even the next.

It was then and there that Justin decided to re-download MENAFTER10 and return to the app in new form and no more damn hats.

Only minutes later, a new message welcomed him back.

cute face pic. u got a fat ass?

CHAPTER 3

THE LONELIEST
DOUBLE CHEESEBURGER

Brontae felt like he had left the house without any deodorant because he knew he stank of a lingering loneliness. He hoped that maybe, hidden beneath layers of hip clothing or among his handful of friends, it wasn't bad enough for anyone else to notice. Still, the stench made him insecure when he put his hands up dancing, never lifting them as high as everyone else. Brontae sought only to blend in with the mass of men cramped onto the dance floor, doing neither too little nor too much to be truly seen beneath its blue light.

If Chauncey went to the bathroom, Brontae went to the bathroom. If LeMilion went to the bar, Brontae went with him. Even with the crowd inside the club tonight, he didn't lose track of at least one of them to cling onto and cover up the odor that followed him everywhere.

The Menotaur was the place to be on Friday nights. It had been around for at least as long as when he had moved to the city for college. Back then, when he was young and everything seemed new, it had been a mecca for men like him. It was one of too few places where they could be themselves. Everyone went to The Menotaur on Friday nights, so he did too.

Tonight, the line outside was wrapped around the corner with Black and brown gays. And here, lazily twerking in the thick of it, in this place they were waiting impatiently to get into, Brontae, now so very out of college, was thinking of a way he could get out. The Menotaur was like a party he'd stayed at for too long. Nothing and no one were new anymore. Drinking went beyond drunkenness and into numbness.

But Brontae couldn't bear to be the one lame friend that wanted to leave early, the one who was unlike the rest. He'd told himself he would just stay a little bit longer at that party until it died down, but that party had outlasted him by several years. The music had changed just as much as he had over the years. Used to be, he recalled, that Menotaur would play house music on nights like tonight. Now, *that* was his groove. Now, it seemed like they only played house on the fifth week in February. On all the other nights, it was the same trash trap as any straight club. The lyrics, if they could even be considered lyrics, bore no relation to anything in Brontae's life. Brontae didn't sell any damn drugs. He didn't own a gun, let alone know how to shoot one. And there was the same bad bitch with a wet pussy and a fat ass in every song it seemed.

But everyone else liked it. Everyone else was popping, locking, dropping, and flopping their asses all over the dance floor. And so did Brontae.

But Brontae lacked their conviction. What everyone else heard as anthems, he only heard as one loud loop, barely able to tell where one song stopped and the next began.

Brontae was alone in the Black gay world that he lived in. Most of the guys he met these days had the conversational skills of a stapler. He'd tried to love a man or two in his life thus far but he never could love them more than they loved themselves. They weren't looking to date. They were looking for a glorified follower, someone who was subscribed to them for sex and was supportive of their needs and their interests.

It was sad to see what had become of the Black gay world. That world that Brontae had once desperately escaped to had become so shallow and small in the few years he'd spent in it— years that felt like lifetimes—it seemed to fit inside The Menotaur. He told himself he had to get out before it was too late.

"Bitch, it's hot as shit!" LeMilion shouted over the melody of mumble rap, dramatically sucking in a breath of the club's limited supply of air.

LeMilion was a long-legged, lean queen with an ombré fade that was constantly changing colors. Tonight it was fruit-punch red. The profuse amount of sweat on his forehead was sticking to his foundation.

"Um, your face is leaking, my love," Brontae told him as quietly as he could over the noise, handing him the soggy bar napkin stuck to his drink.

"Shit. And here I was thinkin' I was lookin' cute." LeMilion patted his face in an exaggerated panic. "C'mon, come to tha bathroom wit' me."

Brontae blew out his breath, realizing he'd just given him another excuse to go to the bathroom and going to the bathroom meant it was time for another bump. According to Brontae's count, LeMilion had made three trips in less than an hour already.

"Where's Chauncey?" Brontae asked.

"Don't worry. He don't miss a beat and he damn sure don't ever miss a bump," LeMilion said in a sassy Southern drawl.

Brontae followed LeMilion as he broke through the mass and made a way through for the two of them with his height and attitude and presence alone. The club respected him and parted where needed. Brontae squeezed through these gaps as best he could but trailed behind. The club did not see him in the same way as it did LeMilion. It took advantage of his lesser height, lesser presence, almost as if it didn't even see him at all. It stepped on his new shoes. It clipped his shoulder. It nearly knocked the drink right out of his hand.

By the time he made it inside the bathroom, Brontae had almost gotten into two fights. The bathroom was a small club-within-the-club, where loose cigarettes were sold and where bathroom stalls were packed with two and three people. Everyone here was under the influence of at least one substance. Brontae was neither drunk enough nor high enough to fit in here. He quickly searched around for the stick-shaped friend he needed to arm himself with so as not to stand out. When he didn't find him, he played off his panic by posing as someone who actually needed to use the bathroom. He made his way to an available urinal and was about to pretend to piss when a nearby stall door flung open and Chauncey caught him before he could commit to this imaginary leak.

"Brontae, what you doin'?" Chauncey asked, motioning for him to join him and LeMilion in the stall. The invitation was like a lifesaver thrown to a drowning man, and Brontae quickly swam into the stall.

LeMilion secured the latch behind him protectively. "Where'd you go?"

"I thought I was right behind you," answered Brontae.

"Chile, here." LeMilion handed him a key and a baggie of snow-white powder.

That's what LeMilion was there for, Brontae reminded himself, to boss him into either having a good time or at least supplying what he needed to look like he was.

Seeing Brontae clumsily dig out a heap of coke, Chauncey laughed. "Yo' heavy-handed ass. That's almost the whole damn bag."

Chauncey's purpose, on the other hand, wasn't as clear. Sure, he was cute and "slim thicc" and all, but what else was he really? He wasn't funny. He wasn't particularly bright. He wasn't really even a friend, except nights and weekends. Brontae couldn't actually remember the last time he'd seen either of them in daylight. LeMilion was too broke to go see those weird little indie movies starring all those goddamn white people he'd never heard of, so most of the time Brontae just waited until he could find a stream online. Chauncey had gone with him to an art show, once upon a time, but come to think, that was only because he thought it would count as extra credit for that class he ended up dropping out of. And since Brontae couldn't dare show up solo, he didn't make it out to many art galleries and exhibits and film festivals either. But Brontae could always count on them come Friday night because there was always some club or some party that they all could go to. Now, standing beside them after five years of Friday nights, crammed inside a disgusting bathroom stall, Brontae could see how very far they were from being close friends.

"Lemme get a cigarette. Bitch, I know you got one," LeMilion told Brontae.

Brontae snorted the powder into his nostril before coughing up a menthol cigarette from his dwindling pack. LeMilion's powder was known to be cheap with little more potency than baby powder, especially on Brontae. Mostly, it curbed his appetite, made his nose tingle, and dried his throat. Like the music in The Menotaur, it didn't do anything for him like it did for LeMilion and Chauncey besides strengthen his physical tolerance for these kinds of nights that normally lasted until morning.

"You coming to the afterhours with us?" LeMilion asked.

"Nah. Not tonight," replied Brontae.

"Why? It ain't like you gotta work in the morning," LeMilion pressed.

"I ain't trynna be out that late. I need to wake up early so I can . . . write," Brontae said reluctantly, passing the powder to Chauncey.

Brontae didn't like to bring up his writing. He didn't have many writer-friends and knowing his current company and their interests he knew writing made him seem especially musty to them. To them, writing was a solitary and strange activity. Chauncey had a sharp nose for just that sort of thing. He could smell the stank of Brontae's loneliness like a shark could blood.

"Aw . . . that's right, Brontae wanna write for tha movies. Ain't that right?" he asked with a toothy smile. "A ol' Quentin Tarantino-hoe."

Amused with himself, Chauncey inhaled the coke into his nose.

"Yep. And what about you? Wasn't you trying to be Keesha Keenova's choreographer or something?" Brontae shot back. "Well, do tell, how is ol' Keesh and that eight-count coming along? Dat world tour must surely be selling out by now."

"Oop," LeMilion snickered.

"Whatever," said Chauncey.

Brontae had a way with words that his two friends could appreciate in moments like this. Like their friendship itself, these moments were a hybrid of conflict, comedy, challenge, and some unmeasurable camaraderie. Silently, Brontae and Chauncey retracted their claws for now and agreed to go on with the night.

Chauncey got drunk and disappeared with a stranger he'd peeled off the wall, reappearing in sporadic bursts. LeMilion worked in a circuit around the club, beelining from his bump trips in the bathroom to the dancefloor to asking Brontae to borrow another cigarette or another five, ten, twenty dollars that he'd never repay so he could go back to the bar. Brontae followed along to it all, to music that meant nothing to him, to drug-infested bathroom stalls, to the bar where he had to buy his own drinks, to the afterhours, to wherever he was not alone.

"And this week's 'Hot Ass Mess of the Week' goes to Aura Era for this stale-ass song she done released. Aura! Girl, you tried it. Over here, talmbout some 'Love on Me Baby' wit' a beat clappin' on da one and da three. Aura, my love, that ain't T, bae-bee!"

Brontae chuckled at his computer. He could always count on the guilty pleasure that was the *Malicious Matters* podcast to get him through a day of corporate slavery. Malicious made it a little easier to put numbers and spreadsheets on the screen that Brontae would rather be filling with dialogue and descriptions and characters and worlds that were not washed out in unfriendly fluorescent lighting like his was, forty-plus hours each week. He was capable of so much more than what he was doing, he said to himself as he stared into the computer's white light and realized, so was his computer.

"Have a good weekend, Brontae," Erin from HR said as she whizzed past his cubicle.

"Same to you, too," he said as she rushed out. Brontae sat there, in his square-shaped workspace, alone in the office. He would be the last one to leave tonight, not because he had to be, but because he wasn't sure where he would go once he walked outside. Unlike Erin, he didn't have a reason to head out in a hurry. No kids to run home to. No man to meet for dinner.

Friday night had come back fast. Brontae wasn't ready to repeat the mistakes of last weekend, so he ignored LeMilion's text: *u coming out 2nite hoe?*

He left the night that he knew it would be on *Read*.

Brontae did his best to manage being on his own. It was easier if he stayed moving, so he went to the gym and killed nearly two hours there. Then he took the train all the way to Ascension Avenue just to grab a bowl of soup. After he'd swallowed the last of that, he aimlessly roamed the neighborhood with its tidy, well-lit streets that were covered in Christmas decorations.

There were parents shopping for children, children shopping for parents, friends shopping like family. Walking between them, Brontae felt like a nuisance. He stepped aside and let them pass him by every chance he got, eventually following behind in the distance, in the footsteps of love he could only wish for.

No one was waiting for Brontae in his drafty, unlit, one-bedroom apartment, but he didn't let that steal the holiday spirit he'd picked up off the street. He started to unpack the loaded bags of lights, candles, tinsel and other decorations he'd bought on a desperate impulse to make up for the night he'd be spending alone. He had never decorated for the holidays before. Now it was his mission for the night to fill his place with as much tribute to Saint Nick as he could fit in it. He could have used a hand from someone taller than him hanging the lights. And he wasn't quite sure where to pin the stockings, so it would have

41

been nice to have a second opinion on if placing them over the bar made any sense. But with the R&B Christmas mix playing, it was fine figuring out this Friday night for himself. It was almost fun.

It wasn't until he grew tired and stopped, briefly, for a break that the night got the best of him. He looked around at the half-done decorations and the empty corner missing a Christmas tree, just like he was missing a man to help him pick one out and bring it up the three flights of stairs. Then he saw it wasn't Christmas joy he was filling his home with. It was just loneliness in warmer lighting. Discouraged, Brontae put down the web of string lights on the floor and poured himself a drink. He took out a fresh cigarette, threw on a coat, and walked out onto the balcony.

The cigarette entertained him in its short life. Once it died, Brontae pulled his phone out his coat pocket looking for it to give him something else to do. It was late but it wasn't too late to text LeMilion or Chauncey, to go back into places like The Menotaur, where he knew he did not belong. His thumb resisted this temptation and went elsewhere instead.

Thanks to MENAFTER10, there was a man who had made himself comfortable on Brontae's couch now. He had walked in with his back straight, his chest pushed out, and his head held high, like he belonged there just as much as the low-pile rug or coffee table. His sneakers were in pristine condition. His haircut wasn't any older than a day. He looked good sitting there.

Brontae wasn't sure where to begin with him. If he listened to the liquor he'd been drinking, he'd start with the little coat of chest hair poking from underneath that snug shirt. He'd tug at it with his tongue and lick his way down its trail. Or he could just begin with his name. Brontae had met him on MENAFTER10 under the username of blessedbrutha08, but after several messages back-and-forth, he gave him the name Chicoby, pronounced *sha-co-bee*. It was a pretty name and Brontae wondered where it had come from.

"You doing it big for Christmas, huh?" Chicoby asked in a strong, husky voice. He was well-spoken, rarely skipping over any syllables, with an accent Brontae couldn't place.

"Oh, excuse the mess. I just started putting things up," Brontae answered from across the room.

"Festive," Chicoby remarked. "Where's your tree, though?"

"Haven't picked one up yet. I don't usually decorate much for the holidays. Just trying something new. Still trying to figure how people in this city, where next to no one has a car, pick up Christmas trees, actually. Never really thought about it until now," Brontae said, uncertain where to sit in his own house.

Chicoby replied, "Well, everyone has that one friend with a car."

Everyone except for Brontae. LeMilion could hardly afford his rideshares, let alone a car, and Chauncey's ambitions, whatever they were, were almost certainly not on anything that tangible, Brontae thought.

"You want me to turn on a light? I know it's kinda dark up in here," Brontae asked, still standing up.

"Do you want to turn on a light," Chicoby answered, with a period at the end of his question.

So Brontae shut the fuck up and joined him on the sofa. He tried not to feel underdressed in his house clothes, wearing cotton sweats and a sweatshirt, socks with no shoes, and his eyeglasses, while the man next to him was fully dressed in name-brand joggers complemented by a simple black thermal shirt, a thin gold chain necklace, and sneakers Brontae knew for a fact cost a couple hundred dollars.

"Come closer," Chicoby told him in an authoritative voice.

Brontae liked the way he gave this direction. He scooted himself over until they shared the same sofa cushion. It was here, in this closeness, that Brontae got a whiff of Chicoby's scent over the smell of pine cones. He smelled expensive. It was a flexible scent too, balling itself up into Brontae's nostrils until it hit the back of his throat, ever so gently, and rolling itself down into his lungs so that when Brontae exhaled, he would breathe out the man.

"Do you write?"

Brontae was so distracted appreciating the scent of a new man it took him a moment to hear the question.

"Yeah," he answered, looking at the thick, bound script sitting on the coffee table. "I don't know. Just some screenplays and stuff. Not really sure what to do with any of it."

Talking about his writing felt as good as having someone ask about it, and when he smiled it was almost like he was using a new muscle.

"That's dope, man," Chicoby complimented. His eyes met Brontae's and made it clear what he was thinking about next. It didn't have anything to do with his writing. Brontae realized this was where the conversation ended as Chicoby brought his face closer to Brontae's. There would be no follow-up questions about what he wrote or what inspired his work. This was it. It was now time to do exactly what he had brought Chicoby into his home to do. Chicoby slipped his tongue into his mouth, startling him. It wasn't the suddenness that took Brontae by surprise. It was the taste that he hadn't expected. Chicoby, so fresh, so clean, was a smoker. They had something in common.

Brontae did not consider himself much of a bottom. He did it from time to time but bottoming was a full-time job and he already had one of those. He lacked the tolerance to endure the kind of pain that came with having dick constantly inside him and he didn't have the time to watch what and when he ate, douching at the drop of a dime. But over the past three weeks of hookups with Chicoby, he was now bottoming on a more frequent basis. He hadn't expected that to happen, nor had he had expected Chicoby to become a recurring visitor in his bedroom.

On the previous occasions when he resorted to the app, he

never saw the men of MENAFTER10 once the condom was flushed down the toilet. Usually, he was left feeling too used, too regretful afterwards to contact them the next day. As for why they almost never reached out to him afterwards, well, he tried not to think about that. Something about Chicoby felt right though, right enough for Brontae to do what he rarely did and message him after they'd first had sex.

Enjoyed you last night.

The more Brontae thought about it, the more it seemed like some kind of fluke that the conversation that followed his message had resulted in phone numbers not only being exchanged, but saved. He didn't care for casual sex but having it with one person regularly felt like something else altogether. There was something to be said about having consistent dick. Bottoming for Chicoby was almost comfortable now, it hurt less and less, and he became accustomed to the slight soreness after their nights together. It helped that there were not very many of these nights and that each one was separated almost a week apart from the last. That give him some time for his body to recover.

It also helped that Chicoby wasn't massive but quite average, actually. The thrill of being with Chicoby wasn't about fat, flopping penis. It was about the allure of having someone, someone seven years his senior, no less. It was about the glass of slowly melting ice and brown liquor that sat beside his on the coffee table. It was about another cloud of smoke that met with his outside on the balcony. It was about leaving work promptly on Friday night now, even ahead of Erin from HR.

What they had going on was a weekend special, always limited to Friday and Saturday nights. But Brontae had "good morning" and "how was your day" texts that came on restful Sundays, dreadful Mondays and all their other off-days that proved that whatever this unnamed thing was that they were doing, even if it wasn't dating, was something more than just fucking through the holiday season. There was more to it, besides sex. Brontae was sure of that. Tonight would be further proof. Tonight was the first time Chicoby had invited him to his place.

The change of venue inspired Brontae to bring along a bottle of red wine to celebrate the occasion. He didn't know much about wine, but he reassured himself as he proceeded down King Boulevard, that the bottle looked befitting for a fancy, handsomely dressed guy like Chicoby.

Then, there was a pulse from his peacoat—a text from Chauncey.

wyd?

Usually LeMilion was the one that sent these out, the club roundup texts. Brontae had turned them down two Fridays in a row. Maybe LeMilion had told Chauncey to text this time since he was better at putting on the peer pressure. Brontae mentally drafted several replies, none of which would include the truth. There were millions of people inhabiting this city but the waters Brontae, Chauncey and LeMilion swam in were very shallow. If Brontae made the mistake of recklessly throwing out Chicoby's name, it was sure to wash up stuck to some dirty rumor or unclean affiliation. He knew this because he had made that mistake before.

"Lavante? Lavante with the locs? I know Lavante! We used to mess around," Chauncey had said when Brontae broke news of his last relationship.

"Oh, no, girl. You don't want him. He's a fan of Tina, and Turner ain't her last name," LeMilion had told him when he'd exchanged numbers with the cutie from that pool party last summer.

Chicoby's name was too pretty to let them throw dirt on it, so Brontae typed up a lie instead.

Hey! I'm writing right now. What's up?

He should have been writing. He wanted to have been writing.

46

Even if seeing Chicoby was a valid excuse for tonight, there was no real reason to explain why he hadn't been writing regularly.

Chauncey replied as he always did when Brontae brought up his writing.

Ooh . . .
Writing? 4 the wknd? again?
ur weird smh

How was it Chauncey could smell the sourness of his solitude from a text? Brontae wondered, fearing who else might have this ability. Then he reminded himself that even if Chauncey could feel the extent of his loneliness, there was someone in his life now who could change it and if things kept going the way they were going, there would be no more Friday nights that included Chauncey. So Brontae braved 40 degrees of winter cold, undeterred, to get closer to that future. He arrived at Chicoby's slick-bricked building just as a young blonde was exiting, her heels click-clacking down the steps of the stoop as she rushed to her ride. Brontae caught the door before it closed, bypassing the buzzer entirely.

The interior of the building was tastefully minimal. The walls were gray and clean; the carpet was plain and modern with only three colors—black, gray and white—repeating themselves in a neat, swirling pattern. Brontae stood, somewhat astounded by the stillness. Peace and quiet weren't cheap in a city this loud. Impressed, he pulled his phone out to remind himself which of these lovely condos belonged to Chicoby. His journey to unit B3 took him up one flight of stairs, where the second floor of the building was just as serene as the first.

The door to unit B3 was thick, heavy and painted in a coat of solid, uninterrupted black. Brontae didn't like it. It looked like it was too equipped for its job of being a door, a barrier. It was so set in its staticity there was no way of telling if it had last been opened five minutes ago or five months ago and even with the silence in the hall, Brontae couldn't hear any noise escaping from the other side of it. Still thawing from the cold, Brontae's knuckles knocked but the door was nonresponsive.

Brontae gave it a few more seconds before knocking again.

The calmness in the hallway made his knocks ring louder. What was keeping him? Brontae wondered, before consulting with his phone and combing through his last texts with Chicoby.

His last text was less than half an hour ago. *What in hell could have happened within thirty minutes to keep him from coming to the door?* Brontae asked himself.

He followed up on his next knock, his third, by immediately sending an accompanying text.

at your door . . .

He waited for the door to open, for his phone to sound, for a noise besides his repeated knocking that would prove that there was someone, anyone else in the building with him. When that didn't happen, he grew more aggressive. Texts turned into phone calls. Knocking became banging. And the silence led to screaming.

"Chicoby! Chicoby! Chicoby!"

His pleas were answered by only more smothering stillness.

Brontae dropped to his heels, pressing his back to the wall opposite the fortress that was that damn door. Alone in the unfamiliar, unusually quiet hall armed with nothing but a bottle of wine and his cell phone, Brontae wondered whether it was that no one in the building was home or if everyone, everyone else but him, was with someone, warm and asleep in bed.

He stopped counting his calls.

Finally, he hung up and called LeMilion instead.

"Hey, wassup?" LeMilion strained out over a barrage of music.

They were at The Menotaur. Brontae could tell by the stupid song playing.

"Hey, what you doin'?" Brontae asked anyway.

"Bitch, we at The Menotaur. You coming?"

"No, I'm not coming. I don't think I can," Brontae trailed off. Thinking of this option for spending the night only made him sadder.

"Huh? What you talkin' 'bout?" asked LeMilion.

"Nothing," Brontae said defeatedly. "Never mind."

And save for the music booming in the background, the call went quiet.

"Where in hell are you?" LeMilion asked with concern that sounded genuine.

Brontae recognized this as his chance to talk, to confide in his friend, to tell someone what was happening, what was hurting. But just as he spread his mouth open to say something, LeMilion went on.

"You suckin' cock or somethin'?" he added.

Brontae knew his friend well enough to know that he was only joking but became annoyed at him anyway, not just for his bad timing but for everything he had ever said or done to ever keep them from being better friends. *Cock. Bitch. Girl.* Every word LeMilion used to speak to him now seemed dirty, demeaning. Maybe it always had been.

"LeMilion, no. I'm not suckin' no cock. I'm not eating no ass. And I'm not no bitch, so don't fucking call me one. I need to talk, like, actually fucking t—"

"What? I can't really hear you up in here," LeMilion said, strained.

Brontae closed his eyes and took a breath into the phone.

"I'm tired. I'm so fucking tired . . ." he said, sobbing. "Whateva. Enjoy your fucking night."

And LeMilion and the music went away, leaving Brontae on the floor with his back up against the wall in a stare-off with that damn door.

He needed a way out from this world where he had friends but no one to talk to, where he was seeing someone but only at night, where a city so big, felt so small. And the way out, Brontae was convinced, was through that fucking door.

—⁂— —⁂— —⁂—

hey I'm so srry abutt last nite I felt asleep
u mad at me?

He barely bothered to punctuate. He didn't care enough for capitalization either. Chicoby could only give Brontae his misspelled sorries for what had happened.

Brontae wanted to send back a flurry of "fuck you's" but he stopped himself. There was a better move he could make that would not just call Chicoby out on his bullshit excuse but would put him in a complete checkmate with nowhere to go that Brontae didn't want him to go.

Why are you playing games?

It was a straightforward question impossible to evade and the five words demanded more from Chicoby than a yes or no or badly spelled bullshit. It was some of his best writing, Brontae told himself as he hit *Send*. He went back to hanging the ornaments on the Christmas tree that he'd paid to have delivered. It hadn't been cheap, but he had gotten it done without a car or a friend. He had finished something. What would he conquer next? There was a dusty script on the coffee table that called for attention but not before his phone did.

He opened Chicoby's text quickly, confident that he was about to claim Chicoby's king in the game of chess that was texting. Why was Chicoby playing games? There was no answer good enough to get out of this one but Brontae read it anyway.

I don't know.

Chicoby had countered him unexpectedly. Chicoby was playing games but he was playing without purpose, with nothing to win or lose. Chicoby didn't invent the game. He'd just been in it for too long. He was playing it defensively because it was all he knew. All it took was the right person to come and change the game for Chicoby, or so Brontae read.

50

Brontae was happy he'd put the Christmas tree up since the last time Chicoby came over. This time, there was something in the room that stood just a little bit taller than Chicoby did and was dressed just a little bit better than he was, in gold and silver and sparkly shit. Something that his help, as it turned out, hadn't been needed for.

"You got a tree," Chicoby said, impressed at the glowing, green symbol of Brontae's independence standing in the corner of the living room.

That made Brontae feel better about forgetting the fact that according to MENAFTER10, Chicoby had been active online, even while he had said he was sleeping. Brontae had accepted Chicoby's apology and the weed he'd brought over as amends but when he finally opened the leftover bottle of wine from the night neither of them wanted to speak of, each sip of the merlot tasted just a little more bitter than the last. It took the weed to chase the bitterness away. But it wasn't so much the marijuana that was getting him high, it was the contact. It was putting the same blunt into his mouth that Chicoby's lips had moistened. Whatever foggy place the weed and wine took Chicoby, Brontae would be right there, too.

So they shared a smoke, passing the blunt, touching one another with a tenderness that had never been expressed before now. Tonight, a hug was just a hug. It wasn't them wrestling the clothes off of one another. Tonight, a kiss was just a kiss. It wasn't foreplay. It wasn't two slimy tongues twisting themselves around the other. There was a warmth in Brontae's home that central heat could not give off. It was that, not temptation, that prompted him to take off his shirt.

"I'm gonna take mine off too," Chicoby said.

Chicoby struggled to remove his sweater. Brontae couldn't blame the sweater for being clingy. Chicoby's body had gotten better, harder than he'd remembered it being just last week. Brontae helped him peel off the sweater, lifting it over Chicoby's head with his undershirt stuck to it. There was a tattoo on his shoulder blade that Brontae hadn't noticed before, a name: *Brandon*. Etched into ebony skin, it was hard to tell if the ink was old.

Brandon. It wasn't spelled in big letters or with flourishes. It was just there.

"Brandon," Brontae read out loud. He hadn't meant to. It was the weed that was to blame for that.

"Yeah," Chicoby said simply.

"Who's Brandon?" asked Brontae, genuinely curious.

"That's my ex," Chicoby replied with nothing in his tone to reveal what the name meant to him now or if Brandon was from last year or last week or if he was like the tattoo, still there.

Chicoby had loved someone at least once, so much that he had taken a needle of ink in his name. But Brontae wasn't envious of Brandon and the mark he had made. He was inspired by him and hopeful for what he, given the light of day, could be to Chicoby.

And that was all that was said about Brandon.

So, Brontae let Brandon be and took another drink of wine, the last that was left of the bottle.

A burst of bubbliness hit him and directed him to play music. He only slightly staggered searching for the remote to the TV. He was only off by one button when he tried to find the music station he was looking for, landing instead by inebriated accident on the classic gospel station.

"Shit, this ain't what I wanted," he said, pressing the remote.

"Wait," Chicoby stopped him. "Oh my God. I love this song."

Brontae turned the volume up and listened uncomfortably. He waited for the church choir to come on and judge him, them—two grown men listening to music that was made for God, half-dressed, under the influence of the marijuana and alcohol and homosexuality. But this song did not care about any of that. There was no choir. Brontae wasn't even sure he could make out an organ. It was piano and strings, played slow and steady, like it had all the time in the world. And the vocals were just as tender. They didn't scream or shout in Jesus' name. They sang it like it was new, putting power into each syllable and love into every lyric. What was this song?

The TV credited it as The Clark Sisters' "Jesus Is a Love Song." It was a beautiful title. He'd never made that comparison to Jesus before but after listening to this metaphor repeated in an immaculate harmony of Black female voices, Brontae was convinced he or she had to be a love song. Jesus. Wasn't he the melody we hummed when we woke up on those mornings we had nowhere to be but with the person, or the thing, we loved? Was that what she sounded like?

"Jesus Is a Love Song" was a love song. It wasn't classic gospel. It was written romantically. It was sung with passion, not praise. Brontae wondered if he was wrong for hearing the song this way or if it was that the song was wrong for being so unbridled as to make God into a love song so beautiful it could be appreciated so far outside the church.

Then, there was a voice that came out of nowhere, nearer to him than the music was. It was Chicoby singing along with the sisters, just lightly at first.

Brontae giggled, mistaking the rustiness of Chicoby's tenor for goofiness until it picked up, on pitch. Not only did he know the song, he knew church and he knew it well. There was experience in the way he sang and whatever it had been, Brontae could hear how much he'd missed it with each line of the song. In Chicoby's singing, a part of himself he hadn't used in some time emerged and Brontae was honored not only to see it but to watch it perform.

"Oh shit. You can *sing-sing*," Brontae said, straightening his neck and straining his eyes as if it would somehow turn down the intensity of his high. He wanted to see him, hear him, as clearly as he could.

His voice was better than it needed to be to impress Brontae. It stood out, even amongst the Clark Sisters. There was conviction in Chicoby's voice, where the booming baritone he spoke with went into full tenor, forgoing composure completely and doing not what it wanted but what it felt. With admiration, Brontae watched Chicoby change before his drunken eyes, coming undone, coming closer to him. Chicoby placed his hands on Brontae's waist and, with weed and wine on his breath, sang the song and its pretty metaphors straight into his face. They swayed, drunk and shirtless under the star that topped the Christmas tree, to a rhythm that was so gentle, it was God.

Brontae woke up without soreness, nestled in Chicoby's embrace. It took several seconds for him to remember that they had not done anything more than dance and sing themselves to sleep, ultimately collapsing on the couch together. That had only been a few hours ago. It had been such a special night. Brontae couldn't leave it passed out on the sofa. It deserved to be tucked into bed, neatly. At the very least, it deserved a blanket over it. Brontae carefully detached the arm that was wrapped around his waist and got up to turn off the TV. He took the liberty of gathering their cell phones and putting them on the charger, plugging Chicoby's into his spare, preparing for the morning. He went to the closet and unfolded his best throw blanket, hurrying back to the couch, back to the comfort.

"Damn," Chicoby said, sitting upright, slowly piecing together the night. "What time is it?"

"Almost three," answered Brontae.

"We were knocked tha fuck out, huh?" said Chicoby, writhing his way out from the comfort they'd formed on the couch.

"Do you want to get in tha bed?" Brontae asked him.

"Nah," he said as he slid his sweater back on. "I gotta get something to eat. I got the munchies like a muthafucka."

"Me too," Brontae echoed, making up this sudden appetite to match Chicoby. "I got some snacks and shit in the fridge."

"Don't worry about it. I want something greasy," Chicoby told him, putting back on every layer of clothing that had come off.

"I got some leftover pizza I can put in the oven. Won't take long," Brontae offered.

"I was actually thinking Big Momma Burger," said Chicoby, fully dressed and fumbling through his pockets for his keys.

"That's all the way on Fourth and Forum. Dat's where you going?" Brontae asked. Then, encouraged by the intimacy they'd shared over the past few hours, he dared himself to say, "Let me ride with you."

"Um, s-sure," Chicoby stuttered, knocked back by this unexpected gust of assertiveness. "I'mma go down and get the car then. Pick you up in front?"

"The car?" Brontae asked. "I didn't know you drive."

Dangling his car key, Chicoby smirked.

He was the one friend with the car, Brontae registered.

And suddenly, something as simple as a late night food run seemed sort of romantic.

Not only did Chicoby have a car, he had a luxury car. Like everything else associated with him, it was exceptionally cared for and clean. So, when Chicoby took his hand from behind the wheel and removed a cigarette from the console, Brontae was somewhat surprised.

"Can I have one?" Brontae asked him, ignoring his own pack in his jacket's pocket.

"Yeah," Chicoby replied. "Just be careful. I don't normally smoke in the car."

Grateful for the exception that they were making together, Brontae pulled loose a cigarette from the pack and stuck it in his mouth. Chicoby lit him up without question and cracked the windows so that the smoke could escape the car. The fresh, cool air coming in, combined with the nicotine, was almost enough to give Brontae back his buzz. Brontae knew this route through and through but being in Chicoby's car and comfortably seated in its leathered texture, parts of the city that were so familiar to him now felt new. Before he knew it, his cigarette was done and they had arrived at Big Momma Burger and found a place in the unusually long drive-thru line. Outside the drive-thru was just as busy. Groups were gathered at the front of the building, placing orders at the walk-up window.

"Goddamn, it's busy," Chicoby said.

"It's the club let-out. All the clubs around here close at three. A lot of people walk over here after. There ain't that many places around here that are twenty-four-seven," Brontae explained from experience. He knew this area quite well. They were just a block or two from The Menotaur.

The line moved slowly. When it was finally time to order, Chicoby went with twelve-piece nuggets, a medium fry and soda.

"What do you want?" Chicoby asked Brontae. "I got it."

The double cheeseburger and junior fry Brontae selected from the value menu might as well have been filet mignon. It was an honor for Brontae to have his food, as inexpensive as it was, paid out of someone else's pocket. The cashier stuffed everything into a single bag and the car inched closer to the parking lot exit.

Chicoby sighed in exhaustion. Looking out in the heavily trafficked lot, Brontae spotted a familiar pair of colorfully dressed club-goers: a short guy in spray-on jeans and a lanky one with lavender hair. It was Chauncey and LeMilion, straight ahead. They were here from The Menotaur no doubt, refueling before they transitioned over to the afterhours spot.

Brontae needed them to see him. He needed them to notice that he was in the best car wrapped around the building and that he wasn't in it alone. He searched his mind for a reason to let the window back down and found one in Chicoby's pack of cigarettes. Seeing the sudden break in traffic, he had to hurry so he didn't bother asking if it was okay to take another cigarette for himself. Brontae pressed the window down and dragged on the cigarette for dear life, extravagantly exhaling a swirl of smoke in their direction and in a final, split-second of time, locking eyes with them, flashing a boastful smile. The car pulled out, leaving Chauncey and LeMilion behind with their mouths on the concrete ground. The satisfaction made even the smoke taste sweet and Brontae was beaming in the passenger seat, puffing away.

"Ain't you cold?" Chicoby asked, interrupting his enjoyment.

"Are you? My bad," Brontae apologized, tossing the cigarette out onto the street and shutting the window up.

The quiet ride back to Brontae's block smelled of greasy food and cigarettes.

"Make a left right here," Brontae instructed. "There should be parking around here."

Feeling the car stop at the corner where it should have been turning, Brontae turned to his driver.

"I'mma just let you out. I gotta get back home," said Chicoby, stoically.

"You not coming back up?" Brontae asked, confused. Was it something he had said? Something he had done? The stunt back at Big Momma Burger? Had he seen that?

"I would but shit, I'm so used to my bed . . . I probably won't be able to go back to sleep," Chicoby half-explained.

"I have a bed. It's way better than my couch," offered Brontae.

"Yeah, but . . . you know."

The night was already over. It was now morning. Brontae sat in disbelief, watching Chicoby rewrite an ending to a night that had already happened, an ending he didn't like.

"No. No, I don't. You were sleeping just fine earlier. We both were."

"Shit, we were high," Chicoby laughed.

"We can smoke some more if you want. I got some weed of my own."

"Yeah but . . ." Chicoby trailed off.

Brontae waited for him to crack a smile, laugh again or make some semblance of a joke, but Chicoby's face was as firm and square as the door to his place was.

"Well, what about the food?" Brontae's question was a weak knock against that door.

Chicoby dug into the warm paper bag.

"You got the double cheeseburger and junior fry, right?" And he put the flimsy fry tray and single double cheeseburger into Brontae's lap.

The food didn't sit right with Brontae. "Put it back in the bag so I can carry it up," Brontae told him before taking an exhausted breath.

"She only gave us one bag, though. I don't want this greasy shit to stain my seat."

"Yeah but I still gotta carry my food upstairs," argued Brontae.

"I gotta drive. This shit might spill," Chicoby argued back but with control in voice. The way he wasn't allowing it to rise to a volume more appropriate for an argument bothered Brontae.

"But—"

Chicoby's unwavering stare cut Brontae's words short. Brontae, realizing he wanted a fight with someone that didn't regard him enough to even consider him an adversary, shook his head at Chicoby's insolence.

Brontae put together his best, his last, attempt to save the night from what he could only perceive as nonsense. "Chicoby, what's going on? What's the problem?"

"Nothing. I just really need to go home. That's all. I'll hit you up tomorrow," Chicoby said, straight-faced.

But Brontae knew this was their last good-bye, even if he did not understand why. Chicoby would never call or text him again and he would never let himself, even at his most desperate, ever call or text someone too selfish to give him a paper bag to put his hurt feelings in. Their affair or whatever it was, or had been, had gone out the car with that cigarette. Brontae wasn't sure which cigarette, the first or the last. He only knew that that same thing that made it so easy for them to meet in the first place made it just as easy to never see one another again.

And with that heart-rending knowledge, he opened the car door and shut it back with as much force as the food in his arms allowed, letting it make a sound as final as Chicoby's decision was.

Brontae stood on the block, waiting for the car to drive off carrying the Clark Sisters and Brandon and the most exquisite scent along with every other good memory, however few, he had of Chicoby with it into the night. When it did, he waited for the strength he needed to walk inside the building, up the three flights of stairs. He waited for the limpness to leave his arms so he could carry the only proof he had that he hadn't somehow made up the man that had put him out on the street: the food he *hadn't* paid for.

The fries fell out of his hand and onto the pavement before he could acquire any of these abilities. Brontae watched as they lay stiff, spilled out onto the sidewalk among debris and trash to turn as cold as the night was. The weight in his right hand prompted him to open his palm. Loosely wrapped in thin paper, exposed to the frigid air, was the double cheeseburger. He could feel the heat slowly seeping out of it. Brontae thought of eating it right then and there just to put it out of its misery, but he was already in the odd predicament of being a man left on the street holding a loose double cheeseburger at three in the morning. He didn't have to be a man left on the street *eating* a loose double cheeseburger at three in the morning, especially this double cheeseburger. It was just as wrong for him to eat this double cheeseburger as it was for him to be here with this double cheeseburger, this lonely double cheeseburger. The two beef patties were thin, frozen only a short while ago before being cooked in a matter of minutes and packaged for quick consumption. The two cuts of lifeless meat were separated by a square of cheese slapped between them, only half melted because it was only half actual cheese. No lettuce. Mustard and ketchup were splattered beneath the bun with chunks of diced onion stuck to the bread, which was almost as flat at the top as it was at the bottom.

A most lonely double cheeseburger it was, offering next to no nourishment, valued at just a little more than two or three bucks or, in Brontae's case, two or three fucks.

CHAPTER 4

THE U BE TOOS

A broken heart had sent Brontae right back to The Menotaur and that was a shame, LeMilion thought, but it was where he belonged. LeMilion was sorry he thought that, but it was the truth. Whether Brontae liked it or not, he was one of them—a smoker, a drinker, a same-sex-loving sinner. There wasn't a man or manuscript that could change that so the sooner he learned to stop trying, the better. Look for love, sure, but don't be above settling for lust. Love may have been the better of these two, but lust was much easier to find and, unfortunately, that was just the way that it was.

Brontae was lucky, really, LeMilion thought. There were much harder ways he could have learned that lesson. For LeMilion, things made sense again now that he, Brontae, and Chauncey were back together on the scene, standing in line to get into the club that was like a second home to him.

"Fuck him and his leased car!" LeMilion shouted, hoping his words would help lift Brontae's low-hanging head.

"I don't think it was leased, though," Brontae said.

"You'd be surprised," LeMilion quipped.

"How'd you meet him again?" Chauncey asked, watching Brontae's face for the slightest change of expression.

If Brontae told the truth, that he met him on the app, it would be further proof that he was just as familiar with the fuck fest in the disguise of a dating scene as the rest of them and make him sound cheap, common. If he lied, it was because he was just afraid to admit it. Either response would give Chauncey the chance to gloat, so Brontae kept a poker face and said, a little too quickly, "Through a mutual friend."

Chauncey was on to him and his lie but LeMilion cut in and covered for him, sighing heavily and saying, "Ugh. This line's long as fuck. I mean, is this the only muthafucka open tonight or somethin'?"

"You wanna pay and do VIP?" Chauncey suggested.

"Hell no, it's free befo' eleven!" LeMilion reminded him.

Chauncey looked at his phone: it was 10:54. Seeing that the line's progression was clearly not in their favor, Chauncey let out a heavy sigh of his own to keep himself from telling LeMilion to get his cheap ass off the twenty it was sitting on and just give it to the man at the door.

"I'll pay it," Brontae offered begrudgingly. "Just pay me back."

"Okay, alrigh—" Chauncey started, before he was cut off by LeMilion.

"No. We not gonna let you pay. We finally got ya ass out. We gonna get you some drinks. Get you feelin' good. Get you the fuck over dat nigga and onto the next! Brontae, we got you!" LeMilion said, firm about the fun they were going to have once they waited out the line.

Brontae smiled out of gratitude and nothing else.

Further up in line, there was a guy who was thick in the thighs in the kind of way that made his jeans fit so well he might have been born in them. They were like a soft shell for the taut, succulent meat he carried below the waist, like boiled crab legs begging to be cracked open.

"Ooh, he so fuckin' fine!" Chauncey crowed. Brontae and LeMilion looked at the man who had fascinated their friend. Brontae out of boredom, but LeMilion because he looked familiar. Yes, his thighs were sexy, but where was it that he knew them, him, from? he wondered, combing through his memory.

The app. He still had screenshots of those thighs in his phone, come to think. Applaudmyquadz. That was his username. They'd chatted, once, only once. Why was that? LeMilion wondered, glad he'd had the good sense to screenshot and save the pics.

There was something else, though, something else about his profile that stood out in LeMilion's memory.

Then he remembered: he was one of the U Be Toos.

At that, LeMilion turned his attention to the white van parked outside the club, on the sidewalk, with "DAT STATUS THO" written in fat, red letters across it and wondered what he was supposed to do with these U Be Toos that were out here, "thicc" and all.

The HIV-testing-mobile was Friday night furniture at The Menotaur. It was there almost as often as LeMilion was. Most people paid it no mind, too concerned with getting in the club to use the spare time waiting in line to take a free HIV test. Sometimes LeMilion ignored it. Sometimes he watched from the sidewalk as people stepped in and out of the van, but whether he ignored it or not, on no night did he not know that it was there.

The last time LeMilion had been inside that van had been some months ago. Chauncey had a boyfriend back then, briefly, and couldn't come out due to his preoccupation with the new penis in his life. Brontae was out of town visiting family in Florida, so LeMilion had braved the line alone that night. Being alone wasn't a problem for LeMilion. He was never really alone at The Menotaur, anyway. There was always someone he knew from his partying, be it a friend or a bump buddy, and if there wasn't, he knew how to make one.

That night, though, it was a straight line of strangers. There was no one he even half knew well enough who would let him skip, and there wasn't anyone interesting enough near him to help pass the time with conversation. So initially, out of pure boredom, he watched the mobile testing unit and the young people tending to it. It had been some months since LeMilion had last been tested, more than the recommended three for sexually active gay men. Three months was one hell of a window, really, when he thought about it. A man could make a lot of mistakes in three months.

LeMilion recalled plenty of regrets in his past, but when he mentally skimmed through the recent months, he seemed almost saint-like by comparison. If his negative status had survived when he was at his most hoeish, then surely it was still intact now. His body had given no indication of infection— a winter cold (or was it the flu?) was the worst he could remember when he thought about the last time he'd felt sick. There was no cause for concern that a more recent test result would be any less favorable than the last time, really.

There was always that chance, though, some reason to worry that he couldn't always wash off after a shower, a doubt that dented his pillow when he laid his head down at night. But hell, when wasn't there?

LeMilion said a silent prayer and approached the van intent on relieving himself of this anxiety, for now.

He looked at the man exiting the van, cool and calm. He thanked the nice white lady that was giving the tests and went to the back of the line for the club, eager and impatient just like everyone else. LeMilion told himself that he would be no different.

The white woman outside the van greeted him with a smile that said she was only distributing good news that night. Surely she didn't have the face for telling someone that they'd gotten themselves a disease that didn't come with a cure. She welcomed him eagerly, giving him a clipboard of paperwork to complete.

"Just take a seat and let me know when you're done. I'm Sara, by the way."

The paper, unlike Sara, was quite rude, with line after line of questions, each one more abrasive than the last. As many times as he'd completed the form, LeMilion still took issue with its approach to procuring information.

Name? *LeMilion Meeks.* Age? *28.* Race? *Blackity-Black.* Highest level of education completed? *Stints of community college.* Employed? *Thankfully.* Marital status? *Hopeful.* In the past six months, who have you had sex with? *Men.* Oral? *Of course.* Anal? *Comes with the territory.* Receptive? *Sure.* Penetrative? *More often than you might think.*

There were numbers involved too. LeMilion didn't have much of a head for the mathematics, so where he was asked for totals, he came up with rough estimates instead of adding them up manually. He figured this allowed for some margin of error in his favor.

All done, he returned the clipboard to Sara with the meekness of a middle-schooler handing in a test he hadn't studied for, a shit-show of responses that were bound to come back bleeding of red ink with his every mistake marked.

"Awesome," she said, reviewing his work. "Looks good. You ready to hop in?"

"Ready as I'll ever be," answered LeMilion.

In stepped Sara's coworker. He was Black and gay like LeMilion, tall like LeMilion, around about the same age as LeMilion. They were both even the same dark shade of brown.

"Hey, I'm Keith," he introduced himself. "I'm gonna be administering your test."

His friendliness was a formality. Everything about Keith rubbed LeMilion the wrong way. He didn't like that his test results weren't going to be given by the whiter hands that he felt they were safer in. This was a delicate matter that shouldn't be in the hands, no, claws, of one of his own. Black gays couldn't trust Black gays. His belief was supported by the many betrayals from men who looked and behaved like him. And there had been more than a time or two that he'd done some betraying of his own, too.

"Oh, she don't do the tests?" LeMilion pointed back at Sara, trying not to sound as alarmed as he felt.

"No," Keith answered calmly. "But you can hop in and I'll have you done in no time."

His voice was a little warmer this time. That made things slightly better, but LeMilion didn't like the flush of defiance he read in Keith's relaxed face or the way he widened his eyes, never blinking, when he spoke to him.

"All ready?" asked Keith.

LeMilion had his reservations but he was also ready to finish what he'd mustered up the strength to start. For his own sake, he agreed to keep his animosity to himself and stepped into the van. Keith proceeded professionally, holding the handy little clipboard that would tell him everything the city's Center for Infectious Diseases, in conjunction with the Safe Place Sex initiative, thought they needed to know about test recipient 02641.

But they wouldn't know anything about LeMilion Meeks, country boy from an insignificant small town in Mississippi who had been bold enough to escape to the big bright city before he got fat and had a baby like everyone he'd grown up with. Those people from that dusty town didn't see LeMilion as a hometown hero for that accomplishment. They saw him as a faggot who had fled. Those who had grown up with him in that three street town in Wilkinson County, where almost half the population was kinfolk, had learned early on that the sticks and stones they'd thrown as children never seemed to knock down the tall, knock-kneed punk unlucky enough to live there.

When they asked why he talked like a girl, he showed off that thing between his legs that made him a boy. When they asked why his pants were so tight, he said it was because they were stuffed with all the money he had and their mamas didn't. And when they asked him, after he'd grown to six feet tall, why he wasn't playing on the basketball team or why he didn't even know how to throw a football, he showed them what he did know how to throw: his fists.

LeMilion's fatherless home was set amongst the rampant ignorance of those three streets in the middle of the woods. He had dreams of getting out one day and making a life for himself in the city. He'd aimed for Atlanta but had found a way out by blessed means of a job in this city, working in airline reservations. The move kicked the dust he'd left behind in his hurry out of the three-street town across an even greater distance, so he took the job and didn't look back.

His escape from podunk town was his proudest accomplishment. If he didn't have a college degree, he liked to think that at least he had life experience. That, not some fancy degree, was what mattered more when it came to making it through the past six years here in the city, all on his own. LeMilion liked to think that there was at least one person stuck back in that three-street town who was proud of him for that, if nothing else, even if no one came to his mind.

"So, you said that you sometimes have sex while there is drug use?" Keith asked, abruptly reminding LeMilion of where he was *now*.

The van's interior was a cramped, makeshift clinic almost incapable of containing the two long-legged men. The seats in the back were placed on opposite sides, so Keith and LeMilion faced one another, knees nearly touching with a test tube between them and its timer, quietly ticking. Like the inside of an ambulance, it was lit for functionality, not friendliness, with a kind of severe brightness that didn't bounce on its own surfaces even in close quarters.

"Yeah, but not like that," LeMilion made clear. "Just when I party, sometimes."

And LeMilion liked to party. There was so much he'd missed out on being way out in the country and when LeMilion made it to the city, he made sure to make up for it.

The crime-ridden streets of the Kirkland Commons, the neighborhood he lived in, had seen him arrive clean-faced and with the grassy smell of that backwoods town still on his clothes. He didn't ask for much from their streets besides an affordable place to call home, even if he had to walk there quickly to make it in safely. But Julip Avenue and its gay-friendly neighboring streets saw him when he had started playing in makeup, after he discovered the freedom of anonymity he had in a big new city where no one knew him or that town he'd come from. So whenever he frequented those parts of the city, he gave the streets hair that was the colors of ice cream and shirts, then blouses that seemed to have less and less fabric over the years.

Here, he was just another colorful clubhead. The marijuana, coke, and alcohol Keith was referring to were not problems, as he saw it; they were proof of the prowess he had in the streets. For someone like him who had fled from a three-street country town, that was evolution.

That's why, he told himself, he wasn't as bad as he looked on that paper in Keith's hands.

Now, Keith was asking if he used condoms.

The Darlington Avenues, a predominantly Hispanic neighborhood, knew him as a versatile top that MENAFTER10 delivered when some of its male locals needed BBC. The men he met here didn't let the little twist in his walk or the color of his hair stop him from climbing atop of their backs. As long as he had the Big Black Cock they needed, he could be as colorful as he wanted, in the dark. He liked that freedom. And sometimes, he didn't like to put rubber over his freedom.

It was hard to answer Keith's question about condoms without this context considered.

"Yeah, I use them. Sometimes," LeMilion explained. "More often than not, I'll say."

"But not always?" Keith asked-answered.

LeMilion didn't practice 100 percent safe sex, but he at least liked to think of what he did and when he chose to do it as street-safe sex. It was more a matter of discernment than a matter of fact. That didn't make him a raw-dogging rookie, no matter how Keith read his responses.

"What about oral sex? Do you have protected oral sex?" Keith, unblinking, asked.

"Suckin' ain't fuckin'."

The words rolled off LeMilion's tongue before he realized

what he'd said. He did not regret it. Sucking dick was safe sex, for *them*. And LeMilion knew that they both knew that. He could understand that the man was just doing his job, checking off boxes, but it still annoyed him.

The test's timer sounded at this exact moment. Keith put down the clipboard and tended to the test tube.

"Okay. Well, just to let you know that based on your responses, you would be what we consider 'at risk' for HIV and/ or other sexually transmitted diseases. Not to scare you or anything, but things like drug use, even marijuana, and irregular condom use are what we consider 'at-risk behaviors.' We do recommend protection methods such as condoms, even during oral sex, as well as pre-exposure medication such as PreX. Never can be too safe out here. You know?"

LeMilion was unmoved at this monologue and only nodded to let Keith know that the script he clearly had been trained to recite had, at the very least, been heard.

"Are you ready for your test result?"

It was his last chance to not know, but LeMilion was feeling his fate that night and once again nodded in the face of his fears. He wanted them to know he wanted to know.

As Keith studied the test intently, LeMilion studied Keith's face, looking for something between his goatee and sponge twists to give some indication of the results.

"Okay," Keith started, his voice suddenly sweet. It was too swift of a change in inflection, too suggestive of sympathy, so LeMilion knew right then, even if he had not yet heard it.

Flashes of heat overcame him. Though his mouth was open, it felt like he couldn't suck in enough air from the windowless van to cool himself. He felt beads of sweat forming on his forehead but when he touched his face, it was ice cold.

"Your test did come back positive for HIV antibodies."

Hearing it out loud—"HIV-positive"—made him feel even more ill. He felt the color drain from his face.

"You okay?" asked Keith, tucking tissue into LeMilion's hand.

"Lord," LeMilion let out. His mouth was only strong enough to form single-syllable words. So he cried "Lord" over and over until Keith put a bottle of room-temperature water into his hands.

LeMilion sat still, fearful of a new future for himself. From now on, when he woke up every morning and stretched to get his blood running, the virus would be running right along with it through his body. When he went to the bathroom afterwards for his first piss of the day, it would no longer just be his morning piss. It would be his morning piss mixed with HIV antibodies.

His body would never be the same. His life would never be the same, however much was left of it.

How could you be such a fucking dumbass? he asked, screaming loudly at himself in his head.

He was too smart on these streets to be so stupid as to let them get him sick.

He couldn't go back to that three-street town. He didn't want to die there. He didn't want to die.

"Are you okay?"

LeMilion remained frozen in place as his thoughts kept running. He had one more strike against him, his third. Now, not only was he Black and gay but now he was Black and gay and HIV-positive. And unlike the two adversities that had preceded it, this one had been preventable. He wasn't born into this one. *He* had made this most permanent mark on his own life. And for that, he blamed himself and always would.

But there was a part of LeMilion that wasn't mad about it, that wasn't so surprised. He'd heard where a lifestyle like his led to. The naysayers back in Mississippi had made sure he'd known where the road outside town led people like him. So maybe this mark he'd made belonged there and always had, really. Maybe he had just been waiting for it to appear. At least he didn't have to wait anymore. He would never have to take this test again. Answer all those goddamn questions again. Wonder whether he was or wasn't again.

He was and would always be.

And in that, he discovered a sick sense of relief.

"Yeah," LeMilion started, "I'm okay."

He opened the bottle of water and sipped as Keith went on to explain what the test results meant, what number to call, what HIV used to be compared to what it was today and why he did not need to worry.

"HIV ain't a death sentence anymore."

LeMilion had heard this line before: on the news, in some magazine, mixed up in his self-diagnosis via search engine for the slightest rash or discoloration he found on his body. HIV wasn't a death sentence anymore. Then what was it? he wondered, because he knew it was most definitely something.

He thought of all the other things it might be as Keith went on. If HIV wasn't going to end him, maybe it would just end his sex life instead. Maybe he did still have a future but one that was filled with expensive and abrupt hospital visits instead of the exotic vacations he'd dreamed of. Or maybe he'd be like Cedric, the flight attendant he hooked up with last year. The last LeMilion had heard of him on the streets, he was healthy—undetectable, even. He was also making some extra money through online subscriptions to his bareback amateur porn videos starring him and the next fool to find out about his positive-status.

Was that what HIV was? Something he was supposed to hide? Lie about? Disclose only when confronted? He was too disturbed by his inability to answer these questions to notice when Keith transitioned from exposition to inquisition.

"You should be expecting someone to follow up with you to get contact information for recent partners you've had sex with. I'll give you a form to take with you, if you prefer to just email it back with names and phone numbers. If you want, someone can contact them on your behalf."

LeMilion hadn't considered *them*.

With time, LeMilion could imagine a day when he might accept his HIV status but it was these *thems* that Keith was mentioning he didn't trust. One of *them* had given this to him, after all. The one with the broken English and the ass that got so wet he didn't have to use lube? Or maybe it was the one from MLK weekend with the mushroom-headed dick he just wanted to dip inside him for a quick second? The one who couldn't keep it up with the condom on?

"We would just tell them that they may have been exposed and encourage them to come in and get tested, basically," Keith added.

"So, you won't tell 'em it was me?" LeMilion asked.

"Well, no. We wouldn't just give out your name if that's what you mean," Keith said as he handed LeMilion the form.

LeMilion exhaled harshly and examined it. The paper was asking for too much from him, names and numbers of men he only knew under a username. What he knew about most of them was as blank as the form was.

"I can actually just email it to you instead, if you want," Keith offered. "If you just wanna jot your email down for me."

He wrote down his email address and handed the paper back to Keith with the appearance of confidence in his ability to complete it. If he questioned himself any further, Keith would, too, and LeMilion had had all he was going to have of that.

"Here ya go," he said, deliberately making his voice almost as strong as it sounded before he stepped inside the van.

"Thank you," Keith replied, misreading LeMilion's readiness to cooperate as a bad initial reaction to a positive result that took a few minutes to form into manageable resignation. It was quite common in his line of work and he'd encountered it enough times by now to persuade himself into believing that this was what was happening. Test recipient 02641 wouldn't be one of the ones who required he call someone in, one of the ones who gave him trouble sleeping. He needed not worry. Test recipient 02641 was made of strong stuff.

"Well, unless you have any more questions for me, I think you and me are done. I ain't trying to keep you from getting on with your night," he concluded, playfully. "Just want you to remember what I said and keep on keeping on, ya know. Everything's gonna be okay."

Keith shook LeMilion's hand, making him promise to call the number on the card tucked into his back pocket. He slid open the door and the booming bass from the club and the rowdy conversations from the men in its line welcomed LeMilion and his HIV to the world outside of the white van.

LeMilion had been on this street many times, but he'd never seen it quite from this angle, standing outside The Menotaur with no place in its line. So he stood there, knowing his status but not knowing what to do with it. Take it home and mope?

"Welcome to my face! Would you like to take a muthafuckin' order?!" an angry queen shouted from nearby, surrounded by several vulturous acquaintances. The unsuspecting guy he was speaking to, apparently guilty of looking at him for too long, turned his head and ignored the insult.

It was all so very ridiculous, but LeMilion looked on at the loud line of men. Its size had grown since he'd left it. Where he had stood just a short while ago, someone else stood now. Now there was only room for him at the very end of all these men, at the very back, which when he looked further out, seemed to stretch all the way back to that three-street town.

So, seeing his way to Wilkinson County to his right, LeMilion went left, putting his HIV status into his back pocket to join the card with the number he was supposed to call. He fixed his face so that his head tilted up towards the moon, his nose not in the air, but in the atmosphere. His feet were on the ground but just barely, as he skipped past the angry queen and everyone else in line, wishing someone would dare challenge him. He forced the line to make room for him, so that he would always have a place here, even if he didn't have one anywhere else.

"Bitch, ain't he fine?" Chauncey asked, his eyes still glued to Applaudmyquadz.

LeMilion pulled himself out of that night, out of that van, and rolled his eyes.

"Goddamn. He ain't all of that."

Chauncey rolled his eyes right back at him.

Looking down at the little man beside him with the pretty face and simple mind, LeMilion was reminded of why he couldn't tell Chauncey about the secret he'd left in the van parked just a few feet away. There had been a time when LeMilion had thought he was lucky to befriend a young Chauncey Lee with his unblemished, high-yellow face, thinking he could somehow get light-skinned by association or something. There had been a time when he had thought that since Chauncey had a fat ass and he didn't, it was better to be fat ass-adjacent than fat ass-less. With all the attention Chauncey had attracted, LeMilion had made do with his leftovers, men who wouldn't have otherwise looked twice at him. He had once pimped the pretty right off of him and the boy ain't even know it. Now looking at Chauncey, he saw that same streak of obliviousness. No, he would know nothing about what it was like to wake up every morning with a disease from a night unknown.

"Can we please just pay what needs to be paid so we can get the fuck outta this line, please? It's fucking cold," Brontae said, digging in his pockets.

LeMilion had almost forgotten all about poor Brontae. Tonight was about him, not Chauncey, not HIV. Keeping this in mind, LeMilion looked to Brontae with renewed excitement, snapping back into being the boisterous queen he needed to be for them both.

"Just like a bird to wanna migrate when it's cold! C'mon, chile, let's go!"

LeMilion was about two trips to the bar away from an over-draft fee and Brontae's blues were no closer to breaking. Not only were they more severe than he'd estimated, they were contagious. He had been in the mood to dance just a minute ago but now that he was out on the dance floor, dancing seemed to be just as much of a chore for him as it was for Brontae.

Brontae danced like a pineapple, not made to move, and ridiculous when set to rhythm. Having his clunkiness so near was beginning to kill the buzz LeMilion was still struggling to get. If he was going to be around it for much longer, he was going to need another bump.

"Come wit' me to tha bathroom right quick," he said, tugging Brontae's wrist.

"I told you I'm not doing that . . . *shit*, tonight. Nah!" Brontae shouted over the music. There was noticeable intoxication in his enunciation and although his voice was competing with the blaring music, it won by a little too much.

"I ain't putting no more of dat baby powder up my nose!"

As nice as it was to know that the drinks he'd paid for were potent for at least one of them, LeMilion didn't find his friend's candor to be particularly pleasant. Just what exactly was Brontae implying? It was no secret that LeMilion's coke was cheap but since when was that a problem? Since when did what worked well enough for LeMilion become not enough for Brontae? When had that changed? Who did Brontae think he was now?

"Suit yourself, sweetie. I was just trying to help," he snapped, before rolling his eyes, turning his back and leaving Brontae to fend for himself, knowing that the boy wouldn't last long with that flopping he called dancing before he followed LeMilion to where he wanted him to be. As he cleared his path to the bathroom, darting through the dance floor like he was the biggest fish swimming in the bowl, he saw Chauncey, grinding his behind so hard against Applaudmyquadz that his next shit was sure to come out shredded.

It should've been me, LeMilion thought. Instead, his hot-in-the-ass friend was feeling up on what LeMilion had technically seen first. He was starving for sex. He'd been almost virginal since the van and he wasn't sure he would ever, could ever have sex again. And here was Chauncey dancing up on dick he didn't even need right in front of his face, with a U Be Too, no less.

Sexy, discreet and disease-free. U be 2, LeMilion remembered

Applaudmyquadz' profile saying.

A *read* receipt had told him that while he may have known he was only one of those three things, Applaudmyquadz thought he was none of them.

Then there were all the other U Be Toos.

are u clean? TH0TSand_ideas had asked him online.

yep. Just got out the shower lol, LeMilion had answered cutely. That had gotten him blocked.

In the gym, HIV negative and on PreX. You be 2, seansosaucy19's profile had read.

Masculine, down for freaky, STD-free fun. U be too, read anonymouszaddy's.

Full of life, not a low-key leper and looking to stay that way. U be 2, they all seemed to read.

LeMilion was used to being a bony, no-booty-having, overgrown queen. He never minded that, kind of even liked it, but he wasn't used to being a "dirty" one.

And as long as there were U Be Toos around, that was all that he was.

There was only one desirable way to be, really, and clearly Chauncey was it. Not him. So LeMilion let go of his mental claim to Applaudmyquadz.

As badly as he needed that next bump and that next drink, LeMilion needed an understanding friend even more and it was back to Brontae that he went. Brontae may have been a bad partier but he was a good friend and LeMilion felt guilty for forgetting that. Of course, he could talk to Brontae. He could probably even tell Brontae. *Why hadn't he told Brontae?*

LeMilion desperately looked over the dance floor for his dear friend, not finding him where he'd left him.

Instead, he found Brontae hidden amongst all the people that were having fun, his face as blue as the strobe lights flashing on it. Drunk. Stuck to the wall, his head swaying to a beat that was getting the best of him. LeMilion blamed himself for Brontae's condition. He had allowed, encouraged, Brontae to think there was only one way to be—drunk, high and too intoxicated

76

to be unhappy—and that there was something wrong with anyone who wasn't.

He was a U Be Too, too, LeMilion realized. If he was being honest with himself, he was as much a part of the problem as Applaudmyquadz. Maybe it was too late for him, or even Chauncey, but Brontae? He was Black and gay so life would always be hard. That much LeMilion knew. But maybe, he hoped, it wouldn't be as impossible for Brontae to have a better life as it was for him. LeMilion made his way over to Brontae and placed his hands on his friend's shoulders, bringing his haphazard movements to a halt. Leaning down, LeMilion spoke directly into his ears in a voice that Brontae had never heard before.

"You need to leave befo' it's too late," he said like someone's mama.

His direction was clear. His sentence was complete and left no room for questions.

Still, Brontae's glazed eyes looked up at LeMilion for further clarification.

LeMilion hoped he'd understand from the first-off and that even in his inebriated state, Brontae would read in-between the lines for what LeMilion was just starting to understand himself: Brontae needed to find and follow his own way through this twisted world so that his idea of life didn't begin and end here, in places like this, like it did for him and nearly everyone else he knew.

"Don'tchu have to write in the morning?" LeMilion added.

"Yeah, I guess so," Brontae said, shrugging his shoulders.

"So don'tchu think you need to leave soon so you can wake up early enough to do that?"

Brontae wasn't sure how to respond and it showed.

"Want me to call a ride for you?" LeMilion asked. His offer of paying for his ride home and reasons to end the night early startled Brontae because in five years of Friday nights he'd never heard either of them before.

"Um, no," Brontae started, somewhat awkward but somewhat aware. "I ... I got it. I got it."

LeMilion needed to believe that, just as much as he needed to believe there was some other way of getting to that place in life he'd been trying to get to that wasn't dark or dangerous, even if he didn't know of any. He liked to believe there was one, though. And so, LeMilion believed that Brontae could and would find that way on his own.

They didn't say good-bye. They only sensed it. Finishing his drink in one final gulp, Brontae put it down, along with any pretense of having any reason to stay here any longer than he already had and headed to the nearest exit.

The LeMilion Brontae was leaving behind, carefully watching him work his way through the horde, making sure he got out safely, was a stranger he wasn't sure he would ever see again.

As for LeMilion, he could only hope that Brontae never found his way back here again. Maybe when he got his next paycheck, they could go to one of those fancy art festivals Brontae was always talking about. But rent would be due next payday, so he pushed it back two more weeks after that, until he remembered that the payday after that was a holiday weekend with three whole days to party, then it was rent time again soon after. LeMilion realized that, with the way his paychecks alternated between barely surviving and budgeted thriving, the day he'd be free to see Brontae again was so far away, he could no longer see it happening at all and it made him quite sad.

"Brontae!?" LeMilion called out in a clear voice that penetrated the loud music. "Write good, bitch."

And Brontae, smiling back, took the words with him on his way out.

CHAPTER 5

IT'S SO HARD TO STAY OFFLINE SINCE YESTERDAY

@AuraEra sorry to hear about your recent weight gain. wishing you warm and reheated relevancy during your time of unsightly sorrow.

Malcolm swiped his plump index finger across his phone, scrolling through repost after repost of his contribution to what was currently the number one top-trending hashtag: *#AurasEraIsOver.*

Malcolm Fields, better known to social media as @MALICIOUS, had never even been to an Aura Era concert before but, still, he had a problem with the twenty-two-year-old pop star as of late. Even though the blogs were giving her shit about the below-sea-level sales of her new album and the rumors had her as a total train wreck, someone still needed to point out that unfortunate potbelly she'd picked up, as seen on those brutal beach photos posted on *ShadeBarricade.* Malcolm didn't mind being that person. It was posts like these that got him 25,462 followers. And that number was changing by the second as he kept refreshing his screen. He didn't mind that either, the adulation, the validation, the way the barrage of likes and laugh emojis hit his eyes when he stared into the glow of his phone.

He was lost in this light when the subway tunnel took out

his last bar of signal, yanking @MALICIOUS out of his celebration of Aura Era's downfall and pulling Malcolm back into the pungent reality that was public transit. Unable to refresh his screen, Malcolm put the phone down and lifted his head. He always had service north of Longfellow Station. The rowdy, standing-room-only subway car he'd boarded just a few minutes ago was now down to just a dozen exhausted commuters. How many minutes had passed, exactly?

Malcolm did not know.

He'd done it again, missed his stop, too busy letting his phone suck him into the infinite cyberworld where he lived as Malicious Matters, the self-described "messiest kween on social media," known for his shady commentary on celeb gossip, trashy reality shows and just about any trending topic that his following of petty Bettys (that's what he called them) cared about.

"The concerns of disgruntled nobodies is none of my concern," read the bio on his profile.

It was fine, Malcolm assured himself. The next stop was the end of the line. He would just get off at Longfellow Station and wait it out for the northbound train. It would take some time, however—the trains were already on late-night schedule. He put his phone into his pocket so that it would serve no further distractions, straightened his back and sat up, trying to keep his eyes fixed on the door. His attention quickly wandered. A middle-aged man in khakis gripped onto the subway pole, standing like he either just took a shit or needed to take a shit. Across from him was a young, heavily tattooed Hispanic couple whose elaborate ink work looked better than they did.

The train braked for its final stop just as Malcolm grew bored with his people-watching. He deboarded with the other remaining passengers, immediately taking the escalator upstairs where he knew he'd have service. There was only one bar but that was just enough to check and see that Mary Divine, his idol, had reposted him and that the Aura Era fans were flaming him.

The timeline was on fire, just how he liked it.

sosodeep99: *@MALICIOUS got me over here hollering! Lmao*

shadyDaeDae: *@MALICIOUS go in and let her have! #AuraEraisOVER*

ToniBoredom: @MALICIOUS YAAAAS!!! Eat that lil hoe up! #AuraERRORisOVER

Then, a notification popped up that wiped the smile clean off his face: *low battery.*

The notification was not to be taken lightly. Malcolm decided not to go back down and wait for the next northbound train just yet. Charging his battery was a more important priority, and in pursuit of it, he wandered around the subway station, scouring over its dusty crevices for an available outlet. He finally found one, though badly chipped, near the commuter card machine. Malcolm decided to take his chances and plugged in his charger, hoping he wouldn't die of electrical shock.

"Thank God," he said, surprised he had survived this endeavor but less surprised that the outlet wasn't working.

Slouched over his dying phone, the crack of his hairy behind could be seen by any passerby. His gut spilled out from underneath the 2XL work shirt that fit him snug. Just the act of briefly bending over strained his 300-and-something-pound body and when he stood up, he had to catch his breath. While his wind was returning, he recognized someone dressed in a leopard print unbuttoned button-up with a black T-shirt underneath.

"Justin!" Malcolm called out. Even Malcolm's voice was fat and when he spoke, it was loud, heavy and slightly strained, like his weight was pulling on his vocal cords.

"Oh my God. Malcolm." Justin stopped and stiffly walked over.

It had been almost a year, maybe, since Malcolm had last seen Justin, and even longer than that since he'd last seen Justin without a hat covering his head.

Malcolm could see why.

The man had hired someone to leave an oil spill on his head, trying to cover what was so very clearly a bad case of premature male pattern baldness.

So that was what Justin was up to these days, out here wanting the world to believe that that was hair. How unfortunate for him, Malcolm thought.

"Okay, you look good. You just get a haircut?" Malcolm hugged on the few pounds Justin had picked up over the past year.

Flattered, Justin nodded. To the untrained eye, this illusion of a hairline may have gone unnoticed but Malcolm had an eye for these sort of things, these sort of flaws, shortcomings, imperfections in others. This was his entertainment. With the stark, overhead light above them hitting Justin's poor head at such a harsh angle, Malcolm was thoroughly enjoying himself. He had to look away before he broke out into laughter.

"It looks good," he said with a cringing smile.

Justin thanked him.

The sarcasm had gone right over the poor child's follicle-deprived head. Malcolm grinned and mentally gave himself two snaps for that. God, he was good.

As nice as it was to see Justin, Malcolm couldn't think of a single thing they had in common and he was running out of small talk. He didn't really know Justin. He didn't even follow him on social media. He would have to comb through real life to find something else to say. And real life wasn't a place Malcolm liked to live in.

In real life, Malcolm lived at home with the grandmother who had raised him as her own. The child she had raised didn't like being outside in the heat with the other boys on the block who were always playing rough and teasing him, so she let him stay in the house with her, staring into the TV screen, eating. That boy had always liked watching television and make-believing he was a movie star. As that boy got bigger and bigger off cereals and snack cakes and her constant cooking, he also took a liking to the computer and the new smartphone, so she'd bought them for him. She gave her sweet grandson so much of what he'd asked for that he stopped being sweet. He was downright spoiled, fat, failing classes, sneaking out to meet strange men at even stranger hours, getting fired from jobs, disrespectful, changing majors every other semester, and spending student refund checks on the new this-and-thats. Now, at twenty-three, Malcolm was still on his grandmother's phone bill, paying his part in room and board with promises of the day when his followers and subscribers translated to dollars and cents. Until that happened, he got by on part-time jobs that he quickly changed like they were drawers.

That was how he had met Justin. Justin was supervisor at that store in the mall Malcom had worked at for almost three months. Easygoing. Nice eyebrows. Kept to himself. Malcolm liked working with Justin, now that he came to think of it.

"You still working at Adderdale?"

"No. I left right after you did," Justin replied. "What about you?"

"Oh, I'm at the Wow-N-Whoa over on MLK. I just got off work too. They got me working nights and shit. Ugh. Not for too much longer, though. Yeah, cause you know I started my podcast, right?"

"Wow. Look at you! 'Bout to blow up!"

Justin's enthusiasm elated Malcolm. So long as he was the subject of the conversation, they had plenty to talk about.

"I hope so. I been putting in some extra hours so I can put together my first live show later this year. It's gonna be during Black Gay Pride, alright? So you should come! Oh, let me show you the flyer."

With his tongue hanging out his mouth, Malcolm paraded his phone in front of Justin's face. On the screen was a picture of Malcolm sitting with his legs crossed, dressed in all black, holding a comically oversized book. His cheeks, which were dark with patches of acanthosis nigricans, were sucked in like a fish. His lips, which were big and brown, were pushed out like a duck.

Despite the strong image, Justin concentrated on the text.

"*The Malicious Matters Show: Live*," he read with as much enthusiasm as he could muster. "Okaaay. I'm so proud of you."

Malcolm was too and spent the next few minutes telling Justin why. When he finally stopped a second to catch his breath, Justin squeezed in a statement of his own, just barely.

"Wow. That's so good. Well, as for me, I'm, uh, thinking about going to culinary school, so I been working on my application."

"Culinary school? I ain't even know you could throw down like that. You'll have to let my fat ass have a lil' sample of something! A chef! Okay."

A chef. That sounded so adult but then again, he remembered, Justin was knocking on thirty. Better late than never. There was good money in that, probably. Justin might do good for himself. Might even be able to buy himself a better hairline.

That was if he even finished culinary school.

Nothing was certain, after all.

Malcom had just as much of a chance of getting his big break and blowing up as Justin had of becoming a chef. Next time he saw him, it wouldn't be in some stinking subway. He was going to be on TV, popular and prospering, young and with so much more ahead of him, while Justin would be so much older, cooking over a hot stove in some bougie restaurant at best and still working retail, at worst.

Poor Justin.

"Good luck with that," Malcolm said with fake warmth. "I heard it's kinda hard."

He knew plenty of people like Justin who were finishing college and starting careers while he was doing neither, which they always confused with doing nothing. To them, he was just getting fatter, spending too much time on the Internet while they were growing up, thinking they were better than him. None of them understood, they just judged. Justin was a nice enough guy and Malcolm really did wish a whole world of good things for him but not before he could have it first. And until he did, it was best that Justin didn't go chasing waterfalls and just stuck to the rivers and the lakes and the retail store supervisor salary that he was used to.

Malcolm turned his attention back to the world he held in the palm of his hand and let his comments remind him of how amazing, witty, well-liked he was. He spent the rest of the conversation hearing but not listening, talking but not saying anything worth remembering, slipping in and out between conversations with the person in front of him and the people online.

Justin didn't know what to call this run-in but whatever it was, he decided to end it.

"Alright. Well, I don't wanna miss my train. It was good seeing you."

"Uh huh. You too," Malcolm said mechanically as he was in the middle of typing a nasty reply to an angry Aura Era stan.

Another notification appeared and alerted Malcolm that he was now at ten percent remaining battery life. This instilled fear in him so to preserve his battery, he put the phone a little deeper into his back pocket than he had before. He resumed his mission, leaving the station and surfacing on the street, traveling towards a diner he knew of that was just a few blocks away. But before he knew it, the phone had somehow hopped out of his pocket and back into his hands so he decided to drop just a few more gems on his timeline.

@MALICIOUS: *they say good singers sing from the diaphragm and bad singers sing from the . . . gut*

This was accompanied with a paparazzi shot of Aura Era in a bikini with her belly on full display.

@MALICIOUS: *but why are all the Aura Era fans so mad tho? it ain't my fault Y'ALL queen out here whack as hell, struggling to sell and quickly growing stale.*

He was giving the world bars tonight!
He was so inspired, in such rare form, that he ignored his

third low-battery notification. There was just enough juice left to give the timeline a minute or two more of Malicious. He carefully pointed the camera at himself only from the chin up so that no one would see that he was actually in uniform.

"Good evening, you whores," he greeted his viewers, letting two full minutes pass for his audience to grow.

Once he had a number of viewers he deemed suitable for the somewhat late hour, he started his spill.

"So look, I'mma just take a minute to say this one thing and then I'mma let you girls log off and get the rest your asses need. And this is specifically addressed to the Aura Era stans blowing me up, pressed because your queen stomach bigger than mine. Look, I don't—"

The phone's battery life abruptly came to an end and the screen went black.

It was a rude way to go out, Malcom thought, but the diner's neon sign could be seen from where he was standing, if he strained his eyes. He didn't have much further to go, he told himself as he tried not to pay attention to how suddenly sparsely lit this section of the street was or how awfully quiet it was all at once now. There wasn't even a car coming as far as he could see, just empty road. Having no phone to look at, he noticed how very run-down Longfellow Avenue had become. He didn't remember it being this bad. The street had gone to shit. Sections of the sidewalk were cracked and in need of repair while others were decorated with debris or graffiti.

Someone should do something about that and write a letter or email to the office of the city, he told himself as he stepped over a wet condom.

The street smelled too, like cat piss and sex that hadn't been washed off.

"Aye, brutha, you got any change on you?" called a vagrant slumped against a storefront. The man was aggressively home-less, lying in a bedspread that was so spoiled it had to be responsible for at least 75 percent of the stench in the air.

Normally, in situations like this, Malcolm used his phone to occupy his hands and make it look like he was too busy to stop and reach into his pocket. He supposed he could pretend and take his phone out anyway but since it was dead that seemed sort of silly. Besides, something told him that the man was dangerously desperate to see cash, not a cell phone. So without his prop to avoid direct eye contact, Malcolm turned his head away from the man and instead of spare change gave him the dust of his footsteps as he hurried past him and several other similar camps, stepping over homes built on broken sidewalk.

Why didn't they just get a job? he thought as he rushed toward the diner. *Times weren't that hard, were they?*

Malcolm made it to the diner with these questions in his head. Someone was coming out as he was coming in, collegiate trade, who was nice enough to hold the door open for him. Malcolm thanked the man graciously.

"No problem," he replied.

Malcolm liked a man with manners. He slowed down going through the door, taking his time to enjoy this mighty fine act of kindness. He wanted to think that Trade might have enjoyed it too, watching him from behind, but Malcolm knew better than that. No one ever looked at him in that way and no one ever had. Malcolm had never been approached, had never even had a real boyfriend, in real life.

MENAFTER10, however, was a different story. The app knew what to do with people like him. It took his black gums, pillows of weight, and rectangular ass and brought him men who didn't mind all that so much. He knew his role on the app and acted accordingly, messaging MENAFTER10's less-often-fucked leftovers, mostly consisting of oldheads, grizzlies or face pic-less freaks who were turned on by the things they could only get away with with someone desperate to get what they had to give. The things they had to give left Malcolm with cum stuck to his face and coarse towels that he'd had to ask for to scrub it off with and water that he'd had to run over them that was never really as warm as he needed it to be and blood in his stool and numbers he was never to call again. With that in mind, even as much as he wanted to, Malcolm didn't dare let himself look over his shoulder expecting someone like Trade to want *him*, especially out in public. The sound of the chimes slapping against the diner's door as it swung itself shut was like a confirmation. He caught sight of an open seat at the countertop with an outlet just beneath it, just waiting for him, and it took his mind off his sudden craving for what he couldn't have.

The Marquee Diner was a 24-hour greasy spoon located just a few blocks from the downtown nightlife, which at this hour attracted patrons who needed food to help soak up the alcohol they were under the influence of. Tonight was no different. The diner was predominantly populated by students from the local college and each table seemed to be trying to talk over the other. Malcolm swore he must have been the only sober person in the entire establishment. After plugging his charger into the outlet, Malcolm grabbed some napkins and began wiping off the slight perspiration gathered around his temples. He hoped it would also remove whatever these strange, uncomfortable feelings were that had come over him in the past few minutes.

"Uh uh. You gotta make a purchase to plug in," said the waiter on the other side of the counter, as he dragged a wet towel over the counter's surface in one lazy swipe.

Malcolm eyed the maybe eighteen-, nineteen-year-old. He was offended not only by his tone but also by the obviously fake, hazel-colored contacts that gave him a lion-like realness, while the rest of his face gave bull. The septum ring pierced into that potato of a nose certainly didn't help. *And who on earth was still rocking tongue-rings?*

His face was entirely forgettable, Malcolm deemed, and what was his name? *Kameron? Is that what the tag pinned into that grease-stained apron said?*

"Pay to plug in? Oh, okay . . . It's not that serious, sweetie, but even if it is, you cuh just gimme a apple juice," Malcolm said, rolling his eyes.

"Apple juice? Nothing to eat?" Kameron replied rapidly, sizing up Malcolm's frame before whisking off with the order. "K."

Malcolm was happy to see him go bother someone else with his existence. In Malcolm's opinion, it was queens like that who were polluting the gay scene, making it as toxic as it was. Those young queens, always with their claws out. Did he get paid an extra ten cents above the minimum wage he was surely making to hate on his own kind?

It took a few seconds for Malcolm to realize that Kameron was one of only two waiters working. Upon further inspection, he saw the bathroom was locked, with the passcode to it printed on every receipt, *after* every purchase. There were also signs posted in the diner to ward off the vagrants with warnings of the right to refuse service and how seats and bathrooms were for paying customers only. The pay to plug-in policy Kameron enforced suddenly seemed more reasonable, Malcolm admitted to himself. He still didn't have to have an attitude about it though. And did he not see the shirt Malcom was wearing that proved he was gainfully employed and most certainly not a bum? On second thought, Malcolm got offended all over again and checked the progress on the battery charge in hopes he wouldn't have to stay much longer.

The phone remained unresponsive.

This could take some time, Malcolm thought with a heavy sigh, but hardly able to hear his thought over all the chattering.

"Okay but that ain't what I told you, though," he heard a woman say in a tone sharp enough to cut the half-eaten waffle sitting on her plate.

"Um, I brought you what you ordered, ma'am," Kameron said with no remorse in his voice.

"Don't 'ma'am' me! 'Ma'am' yo' damn mammy. I ain't yo' mammy!"

The woman was livid.

It served him right, Malcolm thought, running around here talking to people all kinds of sideways. Better her than him to be the one to give Kameron the attitude adjustment he needed. She was good at it, too. This was Malcolm's favorite kind of show. He'd seen scenes similar to this on some of the reality shows he watched, recapped on his channel, and never missed a single episode of. Malcolm wrestled with the mounted stool, trying to lift and squeeze so he could sit all of his big weight on top of it, thankful everyone was too distracted to notice him. Once he was settled in the seat, he soon joined them in watching this show play out.

"Just gimme my muthafuckin' money back! Run me my money! You remember how much the shit was, right? Since yo' memory so muthafuckin' good, remember me my muthafuckin' money back!" the woman demanded.

Kameron made an attempt to calm her down, in his own way. "No need to get loud."

Now he was telling her what she could not do. And that was all the permission she needed to go completely hysterical.

"Don't tell me what the fuck I need to do! Plenty of things I could tell you you need to do with yo' gay ass, but I'm just telling you one and dat's gimme my fucking money back! Now wassup?!"

It looked like Kameron was swallowing the spit he wanted to hurl between her eyes as he took a deep breath.

Encouraged by the *oohs* and *aahs* of the neighboring tables, the woman's voice rose to its peak volume.

"Yeah, dat's what I thought! You better twist yo' gay ass back behind that counter and count me my change! If you even know how ta do dat wit' yo' dumb ass. Gimme back my shit so I can get up outta dis ghetto muthafucka!"

Kameron looked out into the laughing crowd. Only moments ago, they had been customers he'd served food to when they were craving late-night breakfast. Now they were barbaric strangers who only wanted him humiliated, insulted or worse. None of his fellow staff came to his aid. Shanel kept her head down on serving food to her own tables and when Kameron looked over to Lawrence, the cook, it looked like he almost wanted to laugh too. Out of desperation, Kameron focused on the big-bodied man and fellow gay at the counter waiting on an apple juice he would never get.

Malcolm didn't like the way Kameron was looking at him, the expectation in his eyes. So Malcolm looked away and, trying to find someplace easier to rest his eyes, picked up his phone. But all he saw in the unlit screen was a reflection of himself. And he didn't like the way it was looking at him either.

Left with no ally, no mediator, and no other choice but to defend himself in front of these strangers pointing their fingers at him, making fun of him, flanking him, Kameron sent a salvo of expletives to his most immediate threat.

"Bitch, you must got me fucked up!"

The woman's apparent boyfriend stood up from his seat, rising to his six feet, two inches, towering over Kameron, and took his insults on her behalf.

"Aye dat's a female! You wanna fuckin' run yo' mouf? Run yo' mouf to a man, nigga, since you so hot! You hot, huh? Since you so hot, hit me, nigga, wit' yo' faggot ass! Hit me! You think you nigga enough to do that? Huh, nigga? Hit *me!*"

It took his taunts for Malcolm to fully grasp that this wasn't one of the shows he'd seen on TV. This was real, so real that it was beginning to scare him.

"Ooh that punk heated, boy. He 'bout to whoop some ass," Malcolm heard someone instigate.

The woman's boyfriend heard it too and was prompted to swing first.

Kameron swung back.

Full-on chaos broke out as the fight went on for nearly two uninterrupted minutes.

Some people continued eating their scrambled eggs and hash browns as the two men went at each other, from wall to window to the tiled floor. Some sipped orange juice and iced tea while tables were overturned and plates were shattered and chairs were thrown and the woman, attempting to pull her man off of Kameron before the cops came, got tangled into the fight and her top was torn and her breasts were exposed.

"*Ratchet Radar*, my nigga!" someone shouted as he pointed his phone in Kameron's face, which was bleeding and missing a septum ring, as it lay stuck in a puddle of blood and maple syrup.

There were others doing the same—young and Black just like Kameron, men, women, some a decade past college and some still fresh-faced teenagers—recording with their phones and looking on with twisted smirks on their faces and nothing in their hearts.

Malcolm was so horrified by them that he wasn't even aware of his own phone when its light returned. His attention stayed on the gushing reality laid out across the floor right in front of him, hurting and in need of help, staring at him, only him, and expecting more. Later, in the flashing lights of police cars and ambulance, Malcolm would finally check his phone and it would be flooded with missed notifications. Among them would be the news that Aura Era had blocked him.

PART 2

CHAPTER 6

EVERY WORD BUT ONE

It wasn't often that Chauncey worked Friday nights, so when he first felt his phone's pulsing alert, he assumed it was someone sending a party invitation he would regretfully have to decline. He was still coming to terms with the fact that he would spend the night chained to the hotel's front desk and miss out on all the fun goings-on, so he didn't even sneak and read the text, like he usually would. He let it sit, unseen, and went on with work. He was an hour into his shift when he got the second, but he was busy with a guest and didn't even notice it had come through. The third one got his attention but, before he could even open it, there was a fourth. They were all from Julius. This was a name he hadn't seen in some time. He wasn't familiar enough with Julius for him to be sending him four texts in a row like this and never had been, really. So before Chauncey even read them, he was uneasy.

> *Hey have u talked to LeMilion?*
> *Can you talk?*
> *Call me*
> *????*

Julius was more LeMilion's friend than his, so whatever it was that he wanted to talk about, *not text,* seemed suspiciously serious.

With nauseating curiosity, Chauncey called right away.

"Hello?" Julius answered cautiously.

"Hey, it's Chauncey. Dis my work phone."

"Oh, hey," Julius said, then he got right to the point. "Have you talked to LeMilion?"

"No."

There was a bit of guilt in Chauncey's voice. He hadn't talked to LeMilion all week, actually, and it had been even longer than that since he'd last seen him. LeMilion hadn't gone out last weekend and when Chauncey came to think of it, he hadn't gone out the weekend before that either. When he added up all the past few weekends since they'd gone out together, it had been an entire month.

"Well, you know he in the hospital, right?"

Julius was going entirely too fast for Chauncey. No, he didn't know he was in the hospital. No, he didn't know LeMilion was sick. No, he didn't know it was that serious. No, he didn't know he was at Christian Memorial Hospital.

Chauncey didn't tell Julius to slow down because it was apparent to him that he just needed someone to listen. Poor thing. He was a nervous mess, tripping on his own words and no doubt confusing LeMilion with someone else. The more he talked, the more Chauncey was convinced that this was all a misunderstanding and knowing what he knew of Julius, more than likely, a drunken misunderstanding at that. So, as he had on more than one occasion before, Chauncey let Julius do what he did best—run his mouth. Before he hung up though, Chauncey had the courtesy to ask Julius to keep him updated on this ailing LeMilion person they needed to pray for and to call him if he needed to talk to someone.

Then Chauncey took a breath. Julius had really gotten him worked up. For a second, he had thought it was *his friend LeMilion* fighting for his life at Christian Memorial Hospital, of all places. His heart had been racing before he came to his senses and remembered that *his friend LeMilion* worked for the airline company and most definitely had health insurance, so he wouldn't be at Christian Memorial—a charity hospital—even if he had a head cold. Besides, *his friend LeMilion* was in good health and had gone with him to that Memorial Day pool party just last month, wasn't it? Sure, he looked a little skinnier, even for him, but he couldn't have been sick because he'd been smoking and drinking and dancing just fine. Chauncey even had pics to prove it. He thought to send one to Julius but he didn't want to be insensitive. Julius was clearly concerned for this other LeMilion person and he couldn't blame him for that. If it was one of his friends, he would have been just as much of a wreck, maybe even worse. Fortunately, it wasn't.

As sad as it was, it was sort of funny too, the more Chauncey thought about it, ignoring the gang of guests at the front desk scratching their heads and blowing their breath, impatiently. They could wait. He needed to call and tell *his friend LeMilion* about this misunderstanding while it was still fresh on his mind. *His friend LeMilion* would let out a big, ugly laugh once he heard about this.

Chauncey excused himself from his front desk duties and walked into the hotel's office where he wouldn't be disturbed. As he waited on LeMilion to pick up, he thought of how he was going to narrate the story. He wanted to make sure he set up the punchline just right, except he wasn't quite sure where the punchline was. No matter. LeMilion would find it for him. He was always good at that.

"Praise the Lord?" a matronly voice answered.

Chauncey wasn't quite sure what to say to that.

"Praise the Lord?" she repeated.

There was irritation in her voice this time and Chauncey realized that "praise the Lord" was her hello, her greeting, her woman-of-God way of answering the phone.

As for why she was answering LeMilion's phone, though, Chauncey had no idea, but he was clearly talking to somebody's auntie or grandmother, so he remained respectful.

"Hey, it's Chauncey, uh, LeMilion's friend. Um, can I talk to him?"

"Oh, baby, he knocked out right now but you know where he at. Don't you? He over here down at the Christian Memorial Hospital. Room, uh . . . 2029."

Chauncey paused, waiting for a prank to reveal itself. When the woman's voice didn't break or burst into laughter, he began to consider what Julius had told him in its actual context.

"Room 2029? Oh—okay. Can you tell him I'm coming to visit?"

"Okay," she said calmly. "What's yo' name again?"

"Chauncey," he said it proudly. He was Chauncey. He was LeMilion's friend. Now, who in the hell was she?

"Oh, I'm his aunt, Mary."

Chauncey wasn't sure if the softness in her voice was part of her down South-sort of speaking or just older age but he didn't want to mistake softness for sweetness.

"I'll see you soon, Miss Mary."

He ended the call and immediately began processing what he had learned. *His friend LeMilion* was, indeed, at Christian Memorial.

He was still trying to believe it when his phone rang. It was Brontae, another name he hadn't had much use for recently. It had been some months since they'd last seen each other.

"Hey, um, did you hear about LeMilion? What happened?"

"I dunno. I just found out myself. He not doing good, I guess," Chauncey said, uncomfortable with his own use of words.

Brontae was all questions. "What happened? Why's he in the hospital? What is it?"

"I'm on my way to the hospital now, but all I know is that he's . . . sick," Chauncey hesitated on his choice of words. "Sick" was all Julius had gone so far as to say and although Mary had been somewhat helpful, she'd stopped just short of saying exactly what it was that had sent her nephew to the hospital.

LeMilion was just simply sick, Chauncey tried to tell himself.

Then, of course, there was *that other word* which might be more applicable, he thought, but Chauncey was in no rush to use it just yet. He knew it would be waiting for him once he got to the hospital.

Chauncey spent most of the rideshare peering out the window, his eyes fixed on absolutely nothing. The city rolled past him in one indistinguishable blur.

Until it didn't. A block or two away from the hospital, the car slowed down, revealing the Katherine Square neighborhood in what was perhaps its ugliest form. Without the grace of the sun, the same Katherine Square apartment building he had remembered as mostly reddish-brown was now just a giant, square-shaped shadow with windows that glowed yellowishly. Under moonlight, it was downright beastly-looking.

Not only had Chauncey been inside that thing, he had once been beneath it. His memory of the sex, the shea butter, and the complete stranger seemed especially sordid to him when he looked at the building now. He thought about the choice he'd had to make inside it. He wanted to remember having real love for himself, enough to know that he deserved real lubricant, not some cheap substitute. But he wasn't able to. He wanted to be thankful he'd at least used a condom, but he couldn't be sure if the shea butter had damaged the latex and broken it or not. He seemed to recall the stranger he was having sex with saying something under his breath about it ripping but they hadn't stopped. Maybe he had lied, Chauncey considered, remembering how bored the stranger had gotten with the constraints of the condom. Perhaps he'd just pulled it off. Chauncey pondered over that possibility, remembering that he had taken a risk, right in that awful-looking building, without really meaning to. Then, there were all the other times since then, when he didn't have the shea butter to blame for throwing caution to the wind.

Maybe he just wasn't remembering it right, he told himself,

turning his head away from the window and to his phone, just as a slew of texts from Brontae came in.

Its boen cancer.
**bone cancer*
Stage 4
I sent his cousin a DM and thats what she said.

Chauncey read them, unaware that he was shaking his head, just slightly, as he did.

Bone cancer. He supposed that was a possibility, if it weren't for the fact that the man he was on his way to visit in the hospital was only twenty-nine years old and as far as he knew, this bone cancer had appeared, advanced, and ailed him in the worst way all in a month's time. Bone cancer didn't work that goddamn fast, he knew, even if, honestly, he didn't know exactly how bone cancer did work. Then, of course, there was *that other word* but the car was nearing the hospital now, so Chauncey left that word for LeMilion to say himself once he made it to Room 2029.

In this city, when bad things happened to uninsured people, Christian Memorial Hospital was usually where they ended up. Being there made Chauncey feel grateful. His life and all of the wild directions it had taken him in had never put him under the care of Christian Memorial.

There was an air of misfortune in the hospital that smelled both sanitized and stanky like old, dirty mop water. Chauncey felt like his credit score was decreasing with each footstep he took down its dull, ceramic-tiled corridors. He felt the absence of his college diploma with each wrong turn he took to find Room 2029. Once he did, he was almost too exhausted from the emotional beating Christian Memorial was giving him to step inside.

He took a deep breath and thought of the friend who would

be waiting on the other side of the door and who would make sense of this nonsensical night and tell him that he was perfectly fine, just needed to eat was all. He tapped against the door and let himself in to see that friend.

The centerpiece of Room 2029 was resting in the bed with his eyes shut. Tubes, so many tubes, crawled out from beneath the sheets, wrapped themselves around his arms and shoulders and snuck all the way into his nose. His face was ashy and unshaven. The fluorescent blond coils of his hair gave him some color but not nearly enough.

Chauncey wasn't sure how to greet LeMilion in this condition. Something told him his usual "hey bitch!" would sound rather harsh in a room like this.

But he had to say something, anything, quickly before he lost the strength to speak at all.

"Hey hey hey. Good evening. Good evening" was what came out.

He let his words, which he wasn't even sure were words, fly out amongst the slow and suppressed humming and pumping of the machines, so many machines, connected to his friend. The words bounced against the lone window with a fabulous view of the parking garage and hit the walls. Chauncey hoped at least one of them touched LeMilion.

"Hey, how ya doin'?" a voice answered.

It came from the corner the closet-sized bathroom obscured, right in Chauncey's blind spot.

Chauncey approached the voice and found a short, plump woman sitting with not one but two cell phones on her pillowy thighs. She was full-bosomed with reading glasses that were almost falling off her saggy face. Chauncey introduced himself.

"Oh, hey, I'm Mary," she said. "Mil, you see ya friend came see ya?"

Mil. Funny that he didn't have any nicknames for LeMilion, even after years of knowing him. The LeMilion he knew thought there was a certain flair to his name and was too proud of it to let anyone skip a single syllable. Maybe, Chauncey guessed, he had made an exception for his family.

Mary's words did not go unrecognized like his had. LeMilion's eyes popped open, revealing a slightly yellow tint and a spark of recognition.

"Chauncey? When … when you got here?" LeMilion slurred.

"Just a second ago. You musta heard me walkin' in."

Chauncey was careful to put color into his every word and kept a smile drawn on his face. But the air in the room grew still and cold and Chauncey's frozen expression of elation eventually waned.

LeMilion exerted the energy to form another question.

"You just got offa work?"

"Boy, how you know I worked tonight?" Chauncey asked in his most upbeat voice as he took a seat in the corner opposite Mary.

Seeing the way LeMilion was fighting to keep his eyes open, Chauncey decided to answer His own question.

"Yeah, they had me working on a Friday night. You know I don't do Friday nights."

"Who … who told you?"

"That you was in the hospital? Um, Julius … Wit' his dramatic self. He said he called your phone."

Chauncey's eyes turned to the second phone on Mary's lap with the gawdy gold case over it.

"Anyway, how you feeling?"

Seeing the discomfort on LeMilion's face, Chauncey regretted asking him that. It looked like just being awake hurt.

"Chauncey, they got me on so much … stuff. So much …"

This was his opening, Chauncey realized, his chance to get the details directly. *What kind of stuff, LeMilion? What's it for, LeMilion? Why are you in here, LeMilion, and when in hell are you getting out?*

Was it selfish of him to ask question after question, none of them particularly easy, to a man who could barely keep his eyes open, though? There was also Mary to consider. She was just sitting there in that corner, wide-eyed and ready to take in every last word, even *that word* Chauncey was looking for LeMilion to say at any moment.

But *that word* was just between the two of them.

The way Chauncey recalled, he'd only heard LeMilion use it just once.

Some months ago, it had been, on a night that went on like a liquid, in a loose sequence of events that had run together, taking no clear shape or form. One moment Chauncey and LeMilion had been at the club, on the dance floor with two strangers grind dancing so hard their sweat seemed to stick them all together in one big mass. The next moment, the four of them had made an appearance at the afterhours spot over on Oxnard Avenue. Then, there had been water at some point. A whole hot tub of it. Shirts that had come off, skin that was suddenly out to be seen and touched and squeezed beneath the steamy, bubbling water. And somehow, after all that fragmented fun, they had all wound up on the floor of some strange apartment.

Well, everybody except LeMilion.

LeMilion had stayed over on the couch with his pants pulled down and shirt still on, watching everyone else wrestle around naked on the carpet.

Chauncey had pulled in quite the catch that night: two sexy exes. They used to date, they'd said, and yet they still lived together in a nice, spacious apartment with mostly naked walls.

"Yeah, get dat pretty ass wet," the light-skinned ex with the sneaky, copper-colored eyes had whispered to the other ex, who was brown-skinned with a centered chest tattoo: angel wings.

That whole room revolved around Chauncey's ass, so much so that it took two tongues to caress it in the way that it deserved. The exes serviced it well, spreading each cheek wide and two-tongue-fucking the taste out of the pretty hole pointed at them.

LeMilion kept his distance, but he was looking at Chauncey's ass with admiration just like the exes were. Ass always was Chauncey's strong suit. LeMilion didn't have the gift of geometrically glorious glutes. He'd been blessed with height but his behind was planted high and shaped to serve no other purpose

103

than excretion. Chauncey's had so much more to offer. Like, for instance, how it seemed to call out for even more attention than it was already receiving when Chauncey threw it back with just enough effort to make it clap against the faces nibbling away at it.

"Fuck yeah!" Chauncey moaned when the sneaky-eyed ex blew the last breath of his blunt into his wet hole.

. . . *Mary*, Chauncey reminded himself, coming out of his mournful daze and inappropriate memory.

He faked a smile and sent it Mary's way.

No, he couldn't tell her anything about what had happened that night. And he wasn't family, so he couldn't ask her to leave the room so that he could speak with LeMilion alone either. Could he? But he had to ask something. His friend was here hurting right in front of him.

"So, uh, what did the doctor . . ." he started before realizing that LeMilion had drifted back under the influence of the aforementioned "stuff."

"In and out, in and out . . . that's how he been all day. He was talkin' yesterday. Shoulda seen him," said Mary matter-of-factly. "But that's what happen when you smoke and drink," she threw in.

Chauncey couldn't believe she'd said it, so he turned and looked into her thick-rimmed eyeglasses for a reason she might have had to say a stupid thing like that.

That's what happen when you smoke and drink? He thought the fuck not. *Stupid bitch. That's what happen when you smoke and drink?!*

Brontae smoked and drank more than LeMilion ever did and last Chauncey checked, he was doing just fine. As for himself, Chauncey couldn't remember the last time he'd been to a hospital.

No matter what she said, Chauncey thought, *a twenty-nine-year-old man doesn't suddenly end up in places like this in this condition, seemingly overnight, because of just smoking and drinking.*

Did the bitch know that?

"Liver cancer . . . " Mary shook her head and let her

words trail off.

Chauncey could see where she was going and that it led all the way to that backwoods town she had come here from. Not only that, but she was trying to take LeMilion back with her. But LeMilion wasn't going anywhere, Chauncey told himself. LeMilion was going to stay right here in this city and he was going to live. He was going to pull through because he just had to pull through.

And as for this liver cancer, yes, that's what she had said, it would just have to fuck off.

Liver cancer, he considered. *So that's what it was.*

He knew that bone cancer shit was bogus.

Liver cancer. That was probably why LeMilion's eyes were all yellow-like. Maybe Brontae had gotten it mixed up, Chauncey thought.

Liver cancer at least sounded better than bone cancer and it certainly sounded better than *that other word* still tucked all the way in the back of his brain. What about it? If liver cancer had done this to his friend, it hadn't done it alone. In pursuit of the other culprit, Chauncey ran back through his memory again . . .

"Ah, hell yeah! Hell yeah, daddy," Sneaky Eyes had cried out when Angel Wings took him from behind and fucked him with familiarity in his forcefulness, driving his dick in as far as he knew it could go. But the whole time he was fucking Sneaky Eyes, Angel Wing's eyes were on the next person in line to get what he had to give. When he saw Chauncey on his hands and knees, his ass tooted up right next to the ass he was currently owning so that their cheeks touched, he got greedy. He sped up. He went too deep.

"Ah, shit!" Sneaky Eyes shouted, arching his back like an anxious cat.

Angel Wings stopped himself and withdrew, allowing Sneaky Eyes some time to recover. While he did, he decided he'd just slip his damp dick into the new ass he'd procured that looked better equipped to endure the pains that came with his pleasure.

Just as the same dick that had just dug into Sneaky Eyes wormed its way into Chauncey, LeMilion called out from the couch, all country-like, "Y'all got some condoms?"

"What?" Angel Wings asked in an agitated breath.

LeMilion didn't mind repeating himself. "Condoms. Y'all got any?"

Angel Wings huffed aggressively at what he deemed disrespectful before he removed himself from the floor and disappeared into the bedroom. The two men, strangers to each other before tonight, were left on the rug naked, on all fours and bewildered while LeMilion, still half-dressed, presided over them like some perverse big brother, touching himself.

"Bruh, fuck is up with yo' friend?" Sneaky Eyes asked Chauncey.

Chauncey wondered the same damn thing.

It wasn't like they hadn't done this at least once before. It had been fun those other times. So Chauncey couldn't guess why LeMilion was being weird, making everyone uncomfortable. Nor did he have a clue as to why LeMilion was asking for condoms he knew he should have been asking for or as Chauncey liked to think, *was going to ask for. Was actually just about to ask for, as a matter of fact*, or so he recalled it.

If he kept it up, LeMilion was going to fuck around and fuck up the fun for them all, and Chauncey couldn't let that happen. Just as Angel Wings returned to the living room and rolled rubber over himself as requested, a phone sounded and brought Chauncey back to Room 2029 . . .

Chauncey knew that sound. He knew it well. It was MENAFTER10. And it wasn't his MENAFTER10. His phone was on silent. It was LeMilion's.

LeMilion was still logged in, Chauncey realized, and someone was hitting him up. It didn't matter who it was. Chauncey knew what they wanted even if they didn't know or care that the man they wanted it from was breathing out of a tube right now. And that was the best-case scenario. At worst, it was a pic of some dick or ass that was meant to be seen by LeMilion, not

Mary. He hoped that maybe she was too old to even know how to open the app. But then, he remembered, he'd seen her playing *Rainbow Lane* on her phone just a short while ago. *The bitch knew how to work a phone.*

Maybe it was locked. But then how had she responded to Julius' texts?

"Back asleep I see," said the new voice coming into the room. It was the doctor.

His arrival took Mary's attention off whatever MENAFTER10 wanted. Chauncey was so relieved someone had stopped her he could almost hear himself exhale. Not only that but finally someone was here who not only knew about *that other word* but also knew what to do about it.

LeMilion squirmed back to consciousness at the sound of the doctor's voice.

Somehow, that hoe still had enough energy to entertain in the presence of a man, Chauncey thought. It was almost enough to make him smile.

"Ah, he's up! How are you feeling?" asked the doctor.

LeMilion let out a faint groan.

"Still sleepy, huh?"

The doctor made this simple question sound like a trip to go get ice cream after school. Chauncey cringed. This white man was talking to his friend in the same tone he'd used to talk to children. And his friend was so weak that he could only nod in the same way that a child would.

"How's the stomach? Still feeling any pain?"

The doctor rolled a white latex glove over his hand and prodded LeMilion's abdomen.

Uncomfortable hearing his friend cry out as the doctor poked at the source of his pain, Chauncey turned his head for somewhere else to look, anywhere else, like the wall where the TV was turned off or the other corner of the room near the bedside where there should have been, but weren't, balloons floating with "get well soon" wishes written across them. The room was dead serious, and made to make clear that the condition of the patient it held in its bed was just as serious.

And so, Chauncey and the room came to an understanding. The situation was dire. LeMilion was dying. If there was a miracle that could be done to save him, at this point, it would be just that: a miracle. The room told Chauncey to plan for the worst and it told him loudly, so loudly, in fact, that he didn't quite hear what the doctor said before he left the room.

Something about some tests, was it?

He was sure he hadn't mentioned anything about cancer and he certainly didn't say *that other word*. Chauncey would have heard that.

"Wait. What did he say?" he asked the room.

"He say they probably gonna have to move him to another room . . . again," Mary answered as she returned her attention to LeMilion's phone.

Chauncey could think of nothing to stop her from doing the inevitable.

"Oh," he said as he sat back and watched her tap the phone.

Then, the phone rang, only it wasn't the one gripped in her hand. It was the other, the one she had been playing *Rainbow Lane* on.

It was her phone and she prioritized it over LeMilion's, setting his back down.

"Praise the Lord," Chauncey and Mary said at the same time as she answered the call, one in a grateful, hushed breath from a corner all its own and the other loud and proud.

"Da cafeteria closed? Well, won'tchu run and get us somethin', den? I'm hungry as can be," Mary went on. "Ain't nothin'. Just me and Mil *friend* here."

The emphasis in her enunciation said so much more than "friend." People Mary's age used "friend" awkwardly, to avoid saying "lover." It had been ages since Chauncey had last heard someone say "friend" like that.

Crazy old fool, he thought. Chauncey could almost feel a smile cracking open the corner of his mouth. He glanced over to LeMilion, looking to share this moment so specific to men like them but found no one in the vacant eyes staring at him—no, *through* him—through the dreary walls of the hospital and beyond that even.

Chauncey thought there must have been something he could do for him. With how senselessly sudden everything had happened, there had to be some unfinished business LeMilion had. Every man had unfinished business. Mary may have been a high-ranking member of the Meeks family but she couldn't settle certain things. Not like a friend could.

LeMilion's whole life was here, in this city, after all, and so were his affairs.

Wasn't there someone he wanted to see? Call? Someone he loved?

Chauncey couldn't answer his own questions.

LeMilion didn't have a man. Chauncey knew that much. There were some man-friends of his he'd met sometime back before but never during daylight. Maybe they weren't serious but surely they meant something to LeMilion now. LeMilion, of all people, was certainly fucking someone. *Wasn't he? He had needs,* Chauncey asked himself. *Didn't he?*

The proof of that came back to Chauncey's mind . . .

It had pointed at him—no, *them*—when he had been on the floor with the exes. It had slanted out of LeMilion's maroon briefs with its one eye and had watched as Chauncey and Sneaky Eyes shared the same dick. A minute or two in one ass. A minute or two in the other. Repeat.

Chauncey had seen LeMilion remove his bikini briefs and stroke himself. That was how he knew that LeMilion wanted the same thing they all wanted. He just needed a little push.

"He just a lil' fucked up," Chauncey whispered to the exes.

And they all agreed to make it easier for everyone by moving the party to the couch instead of the floor.

LeMilion had a body that was strictly business—skin and bones. What muscle and fat it did spare was purely lean. In fact, there was only one place where LeMilion was thick and it was right between his legs—heavy, hard and pulsating. The exes were taken by surprise at what had been hiding behind them the whole time they were on the floor with Chauncey.

It was, by far, the biggest dick in the room.

Dynamics shifted at the sight of it. Angel Wings, the most dominant of the four and the only one on dick-slanging duty for the night, suddenly had the urge to slob on it. He pushed back the coffee table to make room and dropped down to his knees and started sucking on LeMilion's sack as Sneaky Eyes seduced him out of his shirt. Suddenly, they didn't seem to mind the mascara around his eyes and blatant femininity they'd complained about between themselves earlier before Chauncey—the big-bootied package LeMilion came with—convinced them into looking past it. Chauncey didn't take offense to the exes' abrupt disregard for him. He didn't mind sharing.

He was just happy to see a smile on LeMilion's face, except he wasn't sure it was a smile.

It seemed stressed and compressed, almost like a sneeze—a smile that wanted to come out but couldn't . . .

As Mary's phone call tailed off, this puzzling picture in Chauncey's head faded and his disposition changed as he came out of the memory. He'd been there that night with LeMilion. Things hadn't ended well for either of them. Now he was here in this hospital with LeMilion. Things weren't going to end well this time either but Chauncey told himself that, this time, it wouldn't have anything to do with him.

"Well, hurry up and find somethin' for us to eat befo' my sugar get low . . . Alright . . . Bye."

After Mary ended her call, she remembered the nuisance that had disturbed her earlier and picked up LeMilion's phone. Chauncey saw that as a good time to leave.

"Well, friend, I'mma head home," he told LeMilion.

LeMilion croaked, returning back to consciousness as best he could, "Huh?"

"I said I'mma let you get some rest, friend. I'll be back to see you," Chauncey elaborated, trying to make as much eye contact as he could but without letting his sight linger on LeMilion for too long.

He stood up and bid goodnight to Mary, making sure not to look at her directly so that he wouldn't see in her eyes whatever she'd just seen on MENAFTER10.

As for LeMilion, Chauncey wasn't sure what was appropriate. He wanted to hug his friend so tight that he squeezed the sickness out of him like a lemon drained of its bitter juice.

But he had to be careful. And not just because all the tubes and machines were around either. As hard as it was to do, he was going to have to give LeMilion his love with a long-handled spoon because as much as he hated to say it, he couldn't have any of his grave misfortune rubbing off on him. He might have been friends with LeMilion, run in the same circles with LeMilion, been just as gay as LeMilion but he needed to make a distinction to prove to himself that he wasn't some tragic queen like LeMilion. He was only friends with one. So as awkward and uncomfortable as it was, Chauncey made only minimum physical contact when he gave LeMilion his good-bye, mechanically rubbing his hand.

He apologized to himself for that in the ride over to Brontae's that night.

Since they needed help making sense of all the things they'd learned tonight that still didn't make any sense, Julius came over to Brontae's apartment to offer his assistance. Fortunately, Julius kept his ear to the streets. Chauncey and Brontae were both thankful for that, even if they wished it didn't show so severely. Julius had an innate aggression in his voice that, coupled with his Northern accent, made even the simplest sentence sound like a provocation to fight.

Eventually, they gathered that LeMilion had lost his job at the airline a few months ago. Attendance problems, or so Julius had heard. So although he'd kept it quiet, LeMilion had no job, no health insurance, and apparently no money either. They knew that because he had asked to borrow some money from Brontae last month to help with rent.

"Well, what did he say at the hospital?" Julius asked Chauncey, waiting for him to contribute something of use in their investigation.

"I didn't get dat much outta him. He so doped up," was all Chauncey could offer.

"What 'bout his mama? You talk to her?" Brontae asked.

"I didn't see his mama while I was there. Maybe she ain't get to town yet. Just his aunt, and you don't even much wanna know what she had to say."

But they did want to know. They wanted to know as much as there was to know. And Chauncey was bringing them no closer to it. He could see the attitude in their eyes, but Julius went ahead and rolled his anyway just to make his annoyance even more apparent.

"Well, I'mma go see him tomorrow once they tell me what room they moved him to. I'll ask. Somebody gonna have to tell me something," he said defiantly.

"I'll go with you," Brontae volunteered.

"Fine. Go on," Chauncey snapped. "Go see him so you can ask away, since you don't think I did. See how far you get with dat. See what he says. If he can say anything at all."

"No one's saying you ain't ask no questions. Maybe you just ain't ask the right ones," said Brontae.

There was nothing he could say that would satisfy them, so Chauncey let Brontae get the last word on the subject. The sadness he'd seen in the hospital room would be available to them to visit tomorrow. Until they sat down next to it, they wouldn't understand why he was so short on exact details. For now, they settled for what little they did know.

Brontae suggested going out on his balcony for a smoke break so that everyone could get some cool air. Smoking cigarettes only served as a trigger, though, because they all thought of LeMilion and went into recounting all of his outstanding cigarette loans. Each of them had at least one funny story about LeMilion to share and they went late into the night laughing and crying.

112

Chauncey remained calm, though, and whatever emotion their stories stirred up in him, the comfort of Brontae's new Shih Tzu sitting in his lap was sufficient enough to keep his mind off that night with LeMilion that only he knew about.

"I remember that!" Brontae shouted out before taking a drag from his choice of comfort.

Between the three of them, they'd finished a whole bottle of whiskey. Brontae was breaking open a new bottle when Julius realized he'd been so caught up in the conversation, he hadn't even thought to check his phone since he'd come over. As he did, a silence came in and sat between them for the first time that night. The silence took all the talking they'd done and all the ways they had thought it made them feel better and twisted it into something else entirely. By the time its work was done, they realized that they had been talking to no avail at all. They'd only been waiting, albeit loudly, for what they all knew was to come.

Then the silence got up and left with everyone's peace of mind in its possession.

"Hey. Did y'all see this? He posted," Julius said, his eyes fixated on his phone.

"Who posted?" asked Chauncey.

"LeMilion posted."

The three men circled around Julius' phone, staring at a heavily filtered picture of heaven with amber-colored light cracking through a swirl of white clouds that played as background to a centered, italicized quote: "*My home is not on this Earth, I'm just passing through it.*"

Posted by @LEMILIONAIRE two hours ago.

At first, the post gave Chauncey some hope because it meant LeMilion had his phone in his possession and not only that, had good enough strength and sound mind to put together a post, even throw some filters on it.

To him, that was improvement, until he read the words again in their true context. @LEMILIONAIRE was signing off for good!

Julius realized it too and once he did, went back to bawling.

"God, please tell me 'dis not how this boy gonna go out. Please tell me my friend ain't going out like that. Not dis fast. Not to some goddamn lung cancer!"

"Liver cancer," Chauncey corrected him as he handed him a tissue.

"No, bone cancer. Right?" Brontae asked.

"His roommate told me lung cancer."

Julius was sure of himself.

But so was Brontae.

And so was Chauncey.

Silence returned once again and added up all the possible ailments they'd just listed to their true value—nothing—and privately reminded each of them that what they all knew, they knew wasn't something that needed to be said. It was better if it stayed in their hearts.

But the silence was having a hard time convincing Chauncey. He was resistant, opening his mouth to say the one word no one had used tonight. It was just on the tip of his tongue but before it could come out, that night with the exes came back to his mind . . .

LeMilion had been hesitant about letting the exes give him head that night. Sure, he had allowed Angel Wings to roll his tongue over the shaft of his dick but when he had attempted to put its entirety in his mouth, LeMilion had flinched. Chauncey had never seen LeMilion flinch, especially when a fine man was involved.

Angel Wings had been visibly thrown off by this gesture but had been gracious enough to give LeMilion's sack another coat of his saliva until he was more comfortable. Sneaky Eyes sucked his nipples to the point of boredom but was similarly accommo-dating and began working on LeMilion's narrow neck instead.

Since the exes seemed to have no further interest in him, Chauncey needed to find something to do. Chauncey was good at adjusting to just these sort of things, though, and found room between LeMilion's legs, right next to Angel Wings.

There was only one place on LeMilion's dick that Angel Wings hadn't dipped in his mouth and it was right at the tip.

So Chauncey aimed his tongue there, at this untouched territory.

LeMilion jolted up from the couch. "Whatchu doin'?!"

He swatted Chauncey's mouth away from his dick, letting his fingers hit as much of his face as necessary.

"Whatchu doin'?!" he asked, summoning up the same anger in his voice once more. With fury in his eyes, he looked down at Chauncey. "I'm poz, dummy," he spat at him.

"Huh?" Chauncey asked with his mouth hanging open.

"HIV, stupid," LeMilion said, slapping sense into Chauncey with each syllable.

HIV.

He was protecting him, them, from HIV. It wasn't that he didn't want to get off. It wasn't that it didn't feel good. LeMilion was protecting them from him. Maybe a little too protective, the more Chauncey thought back on it, since it was only oral sex, with a low risk for transmission. Chauncey wondered if he knew that sucking wasn't the same as fucking or did LeMilion care too much about him to even take a small chance?

"HIV, stupid."

. . . Chauncey could still feel the sting in his words when he remembered how LeMilion had looked at him with more concern for Chauncey than Chauncey had for himself. He remembered his dick going limp as he looked for clothes to cover himself with, putting a shirt and socks over a night that would never be discussed again.

Looking back, Chauncey realized he'd been so busy trying to forget that night that he never fully acknowledged that he'd been low-key mad at LeMilion ever since, though he wasn't sure if it was because he'd embarrassed him, because he'd never told him prior to then, or because he finally had. That night, LeMilion had made clear, in his own way, that he could no longer do what he was used to doing, tempted as he might have been, scared as he might have been, and untrained as he might have been in doing anything else. If only, Chauncey thought, he had seen it back then the way he saw it now and not let months pass pretending nothing had ever happened, nothing had changed. Asked him if he was taking his medication. Going to the doctor. Doing what he was supposed to do. If he'd just said something, anything, to LeMilion about *it*, his HIV.

As much as Chauncey wanted to say the word now and tell Brontae and Julius what he knew, he felt a burden in his throat when he tried to speak. Maybe it was some kind of bone and/or liver and/or lung cancer. Maybe it wasn't. It wasn't for him to say, he decided to tell himself instead.

So he didn't say anything to them.

"This some bullshit!" Julius screamed out at the whole city from the balcony.

Chauncey stood back and let the night sky, moon and unmoved buildings take the blame for it.

They would visit LeMilion the next morning in his new room located in a part of the hospital that none of them ever knew existed. By then, visitation would be restricted to one visitor for a maximum of one hour at a time. They would bring flowers and balloons and set them next to a LeMilion who would never open his eyes again. There would be no Mary or mother or any other family member or friend when they arrived, nor would there be anyone to replace them when their visiting hour, which they shared in increments, was up. And there would be no doctor available to answer questions about LeMilion's constantly changing cancers from anyone who wasn't family.

But that would be tomorrow's blues.

Tonight, they all smoked in silence, each of them holding LeMilion's last post in their hands as they gave their friend one last *like*.

CHAPTER 7

SOMEBODY'S DADDY

Not only were her breasts plentiful, they were perky things too. They didn't flop to her side and fall into an armpit. It was an impressive feat, considering that the young woman they belonged to was lying across the bed on her back. Even when she wasn't upright, they were. But James couldn't appreciate that and he didn't care anything about her pillowy ass mashed into his sheets either. His attention was hard-fixed on the hole between her legs and nothing else.

He was just about to stick his tongue through the portal that was her pussy into a galaxy far beyond his bedroom when she opened her mouth and almost made him lose his nerve.

"Hee, hee," she giggled. "Why you got it so dark up in here? I can't e'much see."

"I can see all I need to see," he answered in annoyance.

Her silliness was just a side effect of the alcohol. He'd bought it for her. Top-shelf tequila, that's what she'd said she liked. That had been the cost he'd paid to get this prime pussy put in his face.

"Well, I can't e'much see where da ashtray at."

He was doing his best to ignore the marijuana stinking up the room so bad he could barely smell the sweetness of her pussy, no matter how close to it he was. But now that she'd mentioned it, he was all the more bothered by the presence of drugs in his house. He reached over her and grabbed the ashtray from the nightstand so she could ash the blunt.

James didn't smoke but he'd provided the weed too. That had been his other cost. He considered it money well spent. Even in this low light, the view into her was spectacular.

James leaned his face in, slowly, and started sopping up her spongy lining with his big, bubbly, brown lips. Eventually, it returned the favor and its lips coated his mustache with its wet heat. Pussy like this was easy for a man of James' experience. The strip of woolly hair he went to work in posed no problem. He thrived in it.

That was a thing he liked about young women. They kept a manageable coat of hair. Too many times had he been with women—grown women, women his age or at least a decade or so closer to it than this girl was—that had problems with this particular upkeep. James didn't like his pussy buried in over-growth like a rose hidden in weeds.

Not that James discriminated. The hair thing was just a personal preference. He liked pussy of all kinds. Bald pussy. Pregnant pussy. Wide-set pussy. Petite pussy. Bloody pussy. Musty pussy. Married pussy. Motherly pussy. Unmotherly pussy.

He dragged his tongue through her thatch and collected as much of her estrogenic elixir as he could into lap into his mouth. He sank his face further into her, wiping her dripping orifice all over his lips, beard and the undercarriage of his nose. The young woman moaned. Her youth could be heard in her expression of ecstasy, like a bell being rung in the back of her throat.

He had gone through some trouble to get a fine young woman like this in his bed. Young women always required some work, effort, and especially money, but for James, it required a little more tonight. It required that he push back the bad news he'd heard the other day and put his attention on something more pleasant.

Of course, in a town like Jackson, Mississippi, a man with good looks and a decent-paying job down at the chemical plant could have his pickings of the plump women that made up most of the female population. So there weren't many women over forty who would turn down at least one night with James Ross, should he choose to play with women closer to his own age more often and should they be foolish enough to ignore the widely known facts about him and his history of womanizing.

Truth was, James had children older than the young woman in his bed. Usually, that wouldn't bother him. Usually, he'd tell himself that it wasn't his fault most of the women in this gluttonous town had let themselves go and favored mac 'n' cheese more than they did mascara. Usually, he was kind of proud of how he still had a full head of hair with just a little salt and pepper at the temple and, despite decades of drinking, didn't have much of a gut like the sloven fatbacks that frequented the bar the girl bartended at. But in light of the recent circumstances surrounding his son, tonight he felt a little bad about being with a woman who was young enough to be his daughter. So he buried his face and troubles into her until his guilt (or was it grief?) could be laid to rest.

It took thirty-three minutes for him to realize that they could not.

He didn't understand. Pussy was his happy place. How could he be there, so deep inside it, but not be happy? It had always worked before.

So he spent another seventeen minutes trying again.

"Damn. You gon' gnaw my damn clit off," the young woman said, exhausted.

James pulled his face out of her and looked down between his legs. He wasn't even hard. And when he thought about it, he wasn't sure he ever had been since she'd gotten undressed.

He blamed it on her, *always opening up her goddamn mouth, giggling and lighting up more and more of that marijuana. What was the bitch complaining for?* he asked himself. She'd come twice since he'd made a home for himself inside her.

"You got somewhere to be?" he spat his words out at her like chewed tobacco.

"Well, shit, I do gotta work in the morning."

That's what he didn't like about young women. *Always looking out for themselves and no one else. Next, she was going to ask for some money for gas to get home. Always trying to nickel and dime a nigga.*

The phone rang, a new source of light in the black bedroom.

James got up from under her and went to the nightstand to shut the thing up. But as it rang again in its long, shrill sound, he remembered that it was too late at night for this phone call to not be taken seriously. It was happening. He was getting the phone call he had specifically arranged this whole night to avoid. It was a number he didn't recognize but he already knew who was calling and what they were going to say.

He let the phone ring again to give himself more time, more time to wipe the woman off his face, as much as he could anyway. He picked the phone up once he felt his lips were decent enough for conversation.

"Hello," he answered.

"Hey. Dis Lucinda." She sounded like hell. Lucinda didn't say anything after that for a few seconds. Then she did. "Your son just passed."

James held the suddenly heavy phone to his ear as best he could while the rest of him went spinning in the blackness of the room, his mind going dizzy.

His son was dead.

The third of the four boys he had and the fifth of the six children he knew about.

The son that acted like a girl. That one.

That one was dead.

Mil.

He couldn't say that he was surprised. Lucinda, the boy's mother, had called him a week ago to tell him that he was vomiting and couldn't keep any food on his stomach and they were admitting him into the hospital but since he didn't have any insurance, they might need James' help with the medical bills. Things hadn't been looking good. And now he was dead.

"What happened?" James managed to ask amid the warping black room.

He waited, holding the phone closer to his ear.

It took time for Lucinda to answer him. James told himself that maybe it was because she was crying, maybe it was too hard to say it out loud yet.

"Well, dey say it was nothin' else dey could do," Lucinda continued. She didn't outright mention anything about HIV or AIDS, which James knew everyone was suspecting, including himself, but she hinted around it. The way she put it, Mil's death was, in part, a result of him "running the streets too much" and not taking care of himself like he should. The rapid deterioration of his health was something involving a big word he'd never heard of and another one he wasn't sure Lucinda was pronouncing the right way anyway.

"Hmm. So dat's what it was," he said into the phone, faking his own understanding.

"Everythang alright?" the young woman asked in the darkness as she picked up clothes off the floor to cover herself from the melancholy that had manifested itself in the room while she was indecent. Figuring Lucinda must have heard her, James held a finger up to her, a signal for her to shut the hole in her face and be quiet.

"Mmhmm. Well, dey callin' me back—"

"Cinda," he started, with no idea of how he was going to finish.

So he just held the phone and breathed along with her.

"Uh huh. Well, dat's all I wanna tell ya, though."

"Mil," he said. Hearing the sound of his name was just as strange as speaking it. What he said next was as completely foreign to him as Mandarin Chinese. "Mil was a special boy, ya know. Dat's my son and no matter what, I always—"

"Mmmhmm," she stopped him. "I know. Dat's all I wanna tell you, though. I know it's late. I'll be in touch witchu."

And the call ended.

Once James splashed the last of the sex off his face, he sat in the bathtub, soaking in his own dirt but the heat of his guilt made the water too hot for comfort. He sat there in sweaty stillness. He was tired, but this wasn't a night he was going to get any sleep so it was pointless to even try. As time passed and the water's temperature dropped and punished him with coldness and his skin pruned, his cognizance began to slip. The longer he lay in the water, the more he could swear that there was something bubbling up from the opposite end of the bathtub right beneath the faucet and right between his feet.

Something rising to the surface.

Before James could come to his senses, it broke through the surface of the bathwater, popped up, and splashed a distant memory right in his eyes . . .

It was Mil, back when he was a boy. And he was as naked as he could be.

The boy couldn't have been any older than five. But then again, Mil had always taken after him and was tall for his age. So maybe the boy James was remembering being in that bathtub with him back in Wilkinson County had been younger than that. Four or five sounded about right to him. *Yeah,* he convinced himself, he could remember it now. He *was* four or five.

He and Lucinda had long quit each other, not that they were ever really together. It was a bullet he had dodged. He may have made his share of mistakes, but marrying that girl wasn't one of them. Getting her pregnant was, however.

"Quit splashin' dat watuh 'roun, boy," James had shot out at his son.

The bathroom, the only one in the house, had hardly been big enough for one person, let alone one and a half. James had been tired that night and wanted to hit the sheets as soon as possible, so he'd had the boy take a bath with him to save some time. He was living in the shotgun house at the time, just a few yards behind his father's house, James Ross Sr. Everyone in the family had, at some point, spent a spell staying in the shotgun house on Mr. Ross' couple acres of land. James was on his first spell. Before he was even thirty, he had already fathered half a handful of children to the women of Wilkinson County, many of whom he'd known since he was a child.

Seeing the boy still slapping the water, James called out in his booming voice, "Mil!"

The boy made himself still.

Hearing the harshness in his own voice once the boy's name left his lips only made James angrier for having to say it at all.

Mil. That's what everybody called him. But Lucinda had named the boy LeMilion. James wished he'd been around to stop her from giving that name to him. LeMilion was a funny kind of name. And the boy had come out funny too.

"How come I'on see no soap on yo' skin, huh?"

He picked up the bar of soap on the boy's behalf and put it in his hands. Watching him closely, James found himself examining the boy's features—his little nose, his little hands, his little nappy head—and comparing them to his big nose, his big hands, his big nappy head. In his heart, James always felt he wasn't the boy's father. Lucinda hadn't pressed him on his paternity for the first year of the boy's life.

But the boy had grown to develop into a near spitting image of him before he even turned two. By that time, there was no way James could deny what everyone else in that three-street town knew to be true anyway. It was his, alright.

Lucinda put him on child support. And with what she knew he was making at the time, working on cars at the shop, already paying support for all the other children he'd raked up, he had taken that personally.

James was living just outside of town from Lucinda back then. Technically, it was the next town over but the distance between him and his son was several states wide. Of course, he was never too far to get away from the gossip. James was used to what they had to say about him and all the children he had spread out across Mississippi being raised by different women, brothers and sisters who barely even knew they were brothers and sisters, if they knew it at all.

He was no slouch at defending himself, should anyone repeat it to him. But he couldn't stop people from talking. No one was exempt from being talked about. Not even children. Of course, when it came to children, there wasn't all that much to say.

His oldest girl was "pretty just like her mama."

That second son of his did "play ball real good."

But when it came to Mil, they always seemed to have plenty to say.

James only knew how to defend himself against what he knew to defend himself against. He wasn't used to hearing anything about any of his children being different in a way that children shouldn't be different in so when they said things about Mil, he let them say it so long as he offered an explanation as to why the boy was the way he was.

The boy had "sugar in his tank," they said.

Of course he did. Lucinda was always letting him sit up under her and her sisters and her goddamned mama up in that house all the damn time.

"That boy act *just like a* girl," they said.

Go figure. He had tried on more than one occasion to take him deer hunting, but Lucinda was always making excuses. The boy was "scared of shooting." The boy "had school the next day." Lucinda was full of shit.

"That boy a sissy," they said.

He still had time to grow out of it. But James only told that one to himself.

Since James didn't do much more than what the court ordered him to do in regards to his son, Lucinda asking him to watch the boy for the weekend was either a special occasion or utter desperation. She was probably busy working on her next son, James figured.

"Let me see dat soap. C'mon and move down here," James told the boy.

Mil scooched down so that he was no longer backed up against the faucet and was in the middle of the bathtub, close to his daddy.

"Raise your chin up," James told him as he gently rubbed the washcloth over him.

As James went on washing him from front to back, getting him to stand up so he could reach his underside, the boy's attention went into comparing his anatomy to that of this bigger version of him. His chest had yet to develop but his daddy's had some muscle to it, some shape and form. There was even some hair, which trailed down across a stomach that pushed out just a little, with a little softness on the sides. The boy found that kind of funny and he grinned to himself as he kept following the path of hair until it dipped all the way into the bathwater. The boy's attention led him to what was flopping between his father's legs, what he only knew as a "private part." He knew what *his* looked like now but he had never seen what it was supposed to look like once he got big. So he studied his daddy's and was confused by the ring of darkness that circled around it, just below its meaty tip. The wiry bush of hair it sprouted out of was something he couldn't understand either. But what was even further beyond his mental capacity was the way it fascinated him to the point that his own "private part" got big.

James dropped the soap out of his hands once he saw his son's little penis change from soft and innocent into something that was too dirty for him to wash off with his own hands. He tried to pass the bath towel to the boy so he could wash himself, while also trying to pass off what was pointed at his face as something that was perfectly natural.

But the boy wasn't paying attention and didn't take the towel out of his hands. That was when James realized that his son was preoccupied, peering down at *his grown* nakedness. And there was nothing natural about the way he was looking at it, at him.

James jumped out of the tub and covered himself with the first fresh towel he could reach for.

"Whatchu lookin' at, huh boy? Huh?!" he shouted at the boy,

who looked as unsure and uncomfortable about what his body was doing as James was.

"I say what you lookin' at?! Answer me when I speak to you!"

"Nothing," the boy said sheepishly.

That wasn't good enough, so James removed the belt from the jeans he'd thrown on the floor beside the tub and struck him for "nothing."

The boy began crying, another thing James wanted to break him out of, so James lashed the leather belt across his wet behind again.

"Shut yo' cryin'! You ain't s'posed to stare at nobody privates like that! Specially not no damn man!"

But James could still see Mil's erection hadn't gone down yet so he hit him again and again until he could no longer see what he had seen, ignoring the screaming as each lick of the belt sent suds of soap and beads of water flying off the boy's young skin.

Lucinda came the following day to pick him up. When she asked why the boy was red and welted across his back and behind, James just told her that the boy wouldn't mind him.

She didn't ask anything more about it.

The next time she asked James to watch the boy for the night, he was barely young enough to still be called a boy. However, he was old enough for the three-street town to move on from calling him "sweet" or "sissy" and into calling him a "punk," then "faggot."

James spent the years that followed that night hearing about it from neighboring towns and cities outside of those three streets in the woods.

"Mil done moved to tha city," he heard and did nothing.

"You seen dat picture of Mil online? He wearing makeup and everything now!" James heard and did nothing.

"Your son sick," he heard and did nothing . . .

A drip of water fell from the faucet and broke James free from these memories.

When he pulled himself out from the past, there was no boy in the bathtub with him, splashing around because that boy was dead now.

The cold reality of his present was as cold as the bathwater. Even though his fingertips were wrinkled, James gave himself a little more time to sit in it, until he could gather the strength to step back out and do nothing again for one last time.

The first Saturday after his passing, the funeral services for LeMilion Malikeil Meeks were held in the only church in the three streets of town he grew up in. The newspaper posting in that week's obituary didn't include much more information than that, besides his date of birth and date of passing. There was no photo. There was no surviving family listed. And there were at least two misspellings in the three lines of text the Meeks family had paid for.

Brontae, Chauncey, and Julius were the only ones from the city to come all the way to the small town in Mississippi to pay their respects. The rest of LeMilion's friends and acquaintances from the city weren't able to make it because of how quickly things had happened or because they simply couldn't afford to travel the distance.

Chauncey, for instance, didn't have the money to book a last-minute flight but since Brontae didn't want to go alone, he rearranged some of his expenses for the month and paid Chauncey's way. Brontae tried to pass it off as an early birthday present but since that didn't seem like an appropriate thing to call it, he did his best to not think about the dent he'd put into his credit card. But sometimes he did think about it and would look over at Chauncey and wonder what he would have done if Brontae hadn't bought his ticket. Would he have been like all the others and left *likes* and the deepest of sympathies for LeMilion on social media in lieu of paying their respects in person?

In any case, Brontae was happy he was there. The funeral service only consisted of family, friends of family and church members. Brontae, Chauncey and Julius' presence was a testament that LeMilion had friends far beyond this irrelevant town. This gave them some consolation, until they viewed the body and had to look twice to recognize their friend with all the color cut out of his hair, with no earrings in his nose or ears despite all the holes he had pierced in them. He looked nothing like the person he had spent his short life being brave enough to be.

And he never would again.

After the services, the repast was held in the church's small reception room where church members and friends of family had dropped off homemade cakes and pies. Those that didn't had at least brought some store-bought fried chicken or a case of soda to express their condolences. The few that had done even less than that, at least had a "sorry for your loss" or a Bible scripture recital to give the Meeks family.

All James could offer was his presence. He'd driven over an hour from Jackson to even be here, and he'd come just as clean-shaven and suited and booted as any of the brothers from the church, smelling of strong cologne that overpowered any indication of hardship. In case anyone got close enough to catch any of the whiskey on his breath, he had a fresh stick of gum in his mouth. But the thought of the room, full of familiars waiting for him inside, sucked all the sweet out the sugar before he had the strength to open the car door.

There was at least two weeks' worth of gossip for the town to talk about packed inside the church. Most obviously, there was the curious affliction responsible for killing the twenty-nine-year-old man that had been born and raised here. Then, there was his surviving family. His mother was surrounded with the best of their love, their deepest prayers and the warmth of their full-bosomed hugs and kisses, but there were questions about how many of the tears they'd dried from her face were from mourning the loss of her firstborn or from all the branching expenses his uninsured death had brought forth. It was hard to tell with Lucinda. Just about everyone always said that something was always off about that girl anyway.

It was a good thing she had a sensible sister in Mary, they said, who could arrange the services and go and find a decent suit to bury the boy in. Mary was good at things like that. Too good, some people said. Mary had done more for the boy than his own mother.

Then, of course, there was the boy's father.

James sneaked into the church just like the serpent they always knew him to be. The man's guilt was so heavy he could hardly hold his head up to look them in the eye. As it should be. If he had done right by Lucinda and been a father to at least one of his children, maybe Mil would have turned out differently, they said.

There wasn't a move James could make that day that they didn't know about. They saw when Lucinda and Mary pulled him aside to mention that they might need some more money to help with all the expenses, and they'd paid attention to the two of his other children he'd hugged like they were strangers.

"When's tha last time you talk to him?" someone asked James.

The question generated heat that the old church's AC couldn't help with, heat that made the crisp collar of his shirt stick to his neck.

"Been some time, but he was doin' good from tha last I hear," he lied.

They hid their contempt for him beneath the thin veil of holiness that the church required of them and smiled and nodded.

Feeling the heat of the spotlight the churchgoers placed on him, James covertly slipped outside for fresh air and a swig of the whiskey he'd left in the car. To put some distance between him and the church, he walked around back near the cemetery. Figuring that this wasn't properly considered to be the church grounds, James found it a safe enough place to sneak in a quick smoke. He sparked a cigarette and welcomed the nicotine into his bloodstream, letting all of its temporary pleasures tickle the hot knot of emotions he was holding in.

The nicotine was just hitting when James realized he was not smoking alone. Brontae, Julius, and Chauncey, who he only knew as the young men he'd seen in the church during the funeral services, were around the back of the building, just beyond his vision but not beyond his hearing.

"Let's hurry up so we can get the hell up outta here. Dis some sad shit," Julius said.

They didn't want to be here any more than he did, James thought. He knew why he didn't; but what were their reasons?

"I still don't understand," said Brontae. "This ain't no 1992. Don't nobody die like dat from HIV no more, not that fast nohow."

HIV. James wrestled with the word. He'd been wrestling with it ever since he heard Mil was sick. Nothing ever seemed right about what Lucinda or Mary said was wrong with him. His son having HIV and AIDS, or whichever it was, made more sense to him than some cancer but he couldn't blame them for not mentioning it. It would just give people more to talk about and they had already done enough of that. That was why he didn't press them when they told him what it was that killed Mil, even if he knew nobody in this town would believe it. But now, here were three men he hadn't seen before, saying what he was too scared to even think. It was clear to him, judging from their demeanor, that they were the same way as Mil. Gay.

Gay was a word James didn't wrestle with anymore. In fact, in this day and age, he found it impossible to avoid the word, even in Mississippi. Hell, it was all over the TV. He'd even worked with some gay fellows over the years. Why a man would avoid the wonders of a woman's pussy was still beyond James' comprehension but not exactly beyond his tolerance. He'd come around to accepting the concept of being gay over the years and he liked to give himself some credit for that. But Mil wasn't just gay, he said to himself. He was womanly and, apparently, HIV-positive too. And even if he would have come around to all of that as well, the rest of the world wouldn't have.

"It ain't gotta be no 1992, but hell, look around. It might as well be," Julius said with rising anger in his voice. "When gay men die of sickness, people don't ask many questions. They just gossip. The AIDS is assumed. Always has been. Ain't shit changed. We might not die from the shit as much as we used to or as fast as we used to, but we don't get off with just up and dying of the flu, either. No, don't nobody eva believe dat. If you die from the flu, it's only 'cause you couldn't fight it off 'cause of the HIV or the AIDS. If it's cancer, then it's the cancer the AIDS done caused. At least dat's what everybody thinks anyway. Even if they don't say it. If you a gay man and you get sick and die, it's from being gay. Ain't shit changed."

There was a truth in Julius's words that satisfied him more than the cigarette did. He let himself enjoy it a little before thinking of a way to better address Brontae's concerns. "It might not be as bad as it used to be, but it's still bad. There might be more of the girls 'round here taking PreX every morning than there are taking multivitamins but don't let that fool you. People still get this shit and people still die from this shit. And undetectable don't mean unaffected, neither. Hell, we don't even know if he was taking his meds, Brontae. LeMilion ain't tell nobody nothin'."

Brontae, not disagreeing, took another drag of the cigarette. "No, he didn't. And nobody asked nothing either, did they?"

Julius cut his eyes at Chauncey. When he saw that Chauncey was looking even further out into the cemetery than Brontae

131

was, he once again took it upon himself to offer comfort.

"I mean, fuck, I know how to read a bitch but I'on know how to read a bitch mind, Brontae."

Around the corner, James frowned. He didn't quite understand their way of talking to one another. Sure, he got the gist of it but he wanted to catch it all. So he inched a little closer to the corner, his footsteps muffled by the grass, and listened a little more closely.

"We can't blame ourself for what LeMilion did and didn't do. It ain't like he woulda listened to nobody anyway," Julius remembered, fondly. "You know how he was."

There was a smile on Julius' face when he spoke of LeMilion's stubbornness.

"No, I don't know. We ain't really *talk talk* too much. We partied. We smoked. We got drunk. We kikied. There's only so much talkin' you can do with all that to do instead."

There was a finality in this statement that none of them could argue with. Not Chauncey. Not James. Not even Julius but still, he kept a smile on his face as he had just one more thing to say to Brontae.

"You know more 'bout him than you think. Ya know, you ain't gotta know da color of his underwear to know that some of da same shit you go through, he went through. And even if you know just dat, then you know that you knew somebody dat partied, smoked, got drunk and kikied, in spite of all of dat shit."

His words had resonance, even to James, who didn't even know what "kikied" was. In fact, James was a little bit proud now, thinking about how his son had gotten out of this ignorant town and found friends in a place in the world where he could be himself.

"In spite of all that shit? Or because of it?" Brontae added, determined to wipe the smile off of Julius' face.

Once he got what he wanted, Brontae took one more drag and one more look out into the cemetery. He would visit this same cemetery in the woods just one more time in his life. And when he did, he would be carrying a bouquet of flowers to lay atop his friend's final resting place. He would spend nearly half an hour searching the acre or so of land behind the church house for a headstone belonging to LeMilion Meeks. He would never find it, though, because he would realize that his dearly departed friend had been sent six feet beneath the earth with dirt over his remains and no name to be paid respect atop it. By then, LeMilion's social media accounts which were now flooded with tributes and condolences would have waned down to just yearly birthday wishes and commemorations marking the anniversary of his death, remaining dormant until they were deleted due to inactivity.

After finishing their smoke, Brontae and the others walked around the other side of the building back to the front, where the heat had forced nearly everyone inside the church outside.

James stumped out his cigarette. Mil's friends from the big city had come all this way to see him one last time. And not only that but they'd said the most meaningful things he'd heard anyone say since his passing. They didn't belong in that church, just like he didn't belong in that church. They'd known Mil and not known Mil, all at the same time. They had concerns. They had blame. They had their complications with him, and their love, in their own way.

James walked back to the church's entrance and thought to go up to Mil's big-city friends and get their names and thank them for coming. He thought to tell them he was LeMilion's father, to tell them it was nice to meet them, to tell them that they hadn't been alone back there.

But once James joined the congregation, he discovered that he'd been relieved from their self-righteous stares. The spotlight was no longer on him. It was on the three big-city men who stood beneath the closer-to-heaven earth that the people of the church thought they walked on.

Mary welcomed LeMilion's friends into her bosom as she gave them each a hug, but while she did, the rest of the church folk were wondering if they were the same friends that had probably gotten him into the trouble that took him out of this world. They weren't sure which one of them was his lover, but something told them it was the red-boned one with the bright eyes and the big behind. He was probably the one who gave *it* to him too, they told themselves.

James knew what they were thinking and he had half the mind to tell them all to go to hell and stand up for Mil's friends in a way he hadn't stood up for Mil.

But he couldn't stop folks from talking, let alone thinking.

So, James did nothing. He took advantage of this temporary relief he had from their judgment and crept back towards his car. Initially, it was just for another secret swig of whiskey but then it seemed to him that he'd paid his dues for the day. He'd attended the viewing. He'd been there for the burial. Anything beyond that now seemed excessive, pointless even.

So, since he had no further purpose to serve here, he decided he would just go.

Brontae, seeing for the first time that there was a man outside that shared the same face as the friend he'd just buried, was the only one who noticed James as he left one less worry behind.

CHAPTER 8

SOMEBODY'S SON

Elliott's urge for sex began to uncurl itself at a most uncomfortable time for him. He was working another long shift at Christian Memorial Hospital and was busy transporting a patient when his pelvis brushed against the back of the wheelchair, just slightly, and the touch triggered a sensation beneath the thin hospital scrubs. He thought he could piss it away but when he went to the bathroom, his hard-on was still there, making his pee shoot out at all kinds of angles.

It was there when he went into the breakroom to eat and glanced up at the TV. It was only a commercial for men's shampoo, but the men were shirtless, and shampoo and water ran down from thick, silky black and blond hair to the nape of their tan necks to parts of their bodies the TV screen was downright stupid not to show. Once it was safe to rise up from the table, Elliott went back to work. He was informed upon his return to the hospital ward that there would be one less patient he had to tend to tonight.

It was Mr. Landry.

Elliott entered the room and found the bed empty and draped with thin white sheets that had the fresh dent of death in them.

He'd seen stiff, lifeless linen just like it at least a hundred times before, but for Mr. Landry's he had to sit down for a minute and take in the past month he'd had with him.

Mr. Landry was a talker. There was no such thing as just slipping in and out of Mr. Landry's room. Each time Elliott had come inside, he'd come out knowing some piece of what was on his mind. Sometimes, it was just as simple as the weather.

"Hot, cold, rain, snow . . . I swear, you see every season in the same day now."

Other times, it was the sort of thing that was half insult and half inspiration.

"I reckon they don't pay much here in dis hospital doin' what you doin', but you keep ya lil' job now cuz a slow leak'll fill up a creek."

On occasion, Mr. Landry would speak of some of the women nurses, but even when he found it in him to get a little lustful, he never imposed it on Elliott, never asked what Elliott thought about the women or why it was that he never had anything to say on the subject. He didn't even ask if Elliott was single or had children. Not because he was selfish in conversation but because he genuinely assumed nothing. He didn't pick or pry. Most of all, he never really talked about death or despair from sitting in the hospital like so many of the other patients.

That had only happened once, if Elliott recalled, and he wasn't even sure if it counted. He'd simply made a statement. Maybe it was somewhat morbid. Maybe it wasn't.

"I tell ya, you bet not neva' get old."

He'd said it one night after Elliott had helped him with his bath. And he had meant it. The look of defeat on his worn and wrinkled face when he'd said it returned to Elliott's mind.

It was the kind of warning that made Elliott wonder. Wonder why a man who had lived what seemed like a full life with a wife he'd loved until her death and several children and half a dozen grandchildren, even a great-grandson, would say such a thing. Wonder why that same man died not surrounded by any of that family. Wonder how much worse things were going to be for him, when he wasn't just gay, childless and most likely still unmarried but gay, childless, still unmarried *and old* on top of it. Elliott sprang off the bed before his thoughts took him any further into that future. He erased the white board on the wall and prayed that Mr. Landry left the world he had so much to say about peacefully.

"Amen."

When the time came for Elliott to get off work, he didn't have the urge pressing in his pants. What he did have, though, was a long, tiring day of work behind him and a patient who had passed, and so he needed to relieve himself by dropping off his thick, heavy load inside somebody's son. He knew the urge would come back when it needed to.

But who was it going to be tonight?

He opened MENAFTER10 as he left the hospital. It looked like just about every Black man with phone service was online.

His eyes narrowed the selection for him, skipping over everyone who wasn't light-skinned. Then, he popped open their profiles to make sure they fit his next preference: height. They didn't have to be short, per se, just as long as they were shorter than him, which, with his towering height, wasn't much of a challenge to find.

He unlocked his profile for his potentials so that they could quickly understand that it was big dick being offered tonight. Big dick that, because it was big, was most definitely going to get up in somebody's ass tonight, whether it was theirs or someone else's. If they acted fast enough, it could be theirs, but they'd better hurry up before somebody else came and sat on top of it.

Sure enough, they understood.

Now, which one would it be? Who could get to his place the fastest? Who was the sexiest?

Elliott made it to his building before he'd booked his reservation inside some man's guts tonight. He was surprised at how fast he'd made it home, even though the Katherine Square apartment building was just a block away from the hospital. Tonight it seemed like too short of a walk, too easy of a commute—even though that was the biggest benefit of living in this neighborhood. He had been in no rush to get home and had needed a long walk to clear his mind, not the brisk convenience of a short one. So, on second thought, perhaps he wouldn't host tonight.

This reversal came with some repercussions as his options which had just seemed overwhelming began to weed themselves out.

Nigga_noir, as it turned out, was staying with a friend and as badly as he wanted to suck something long tonight, he couldn't host. Neither could fineapple420. Hellayella was willing to host as long as they waited until his roommate left for the night.

Elliott was too worn out from work for the patience to find someone sexy, high-yellow, shorter than him, and stable enough to have a place to host, so he loosened his restrictions a little: whoever would be lucky enough to get his good ol' dick tonight didn't have to be so sexy. Maybe they could just be *cute*. He could work with *cute*. He refiltered his search to cute, high-yellow, shorter than him, and stable enough to have a place to host. Eventually, he settled on the *handsome*, high-yellow, shorter-than-him man with the nice eyebrows, and his own apartment that was only 0.87 miles away from Elliot's.

"My bad. I was in the shower," Justin—or, as Elliott knew him, GOODVIBESGUY— apologized as he stretched the door open.

Elliott walked through reluctantly. "Oh, it's cool," he said as nicely as he could.

Secretly, he was pissed. Not at the ab-less, average-bodied man that had let him in after a full minute of knocking. He was mad at himself for being foolish enough to fall for the deception. There was a full fifteen-pound difference between the man who had made him hard enough to take a quick shower when he

138

had wanted a long one, throw on some clothes and hurry over, and the man who had come to the door in tight-ass shorts and a muscle shirt that showed off muscle-less arms. Elliott forgave himself for moving in such haste that he'd not seen the obvious red flags online: the limited selection of pics, which when he came to think of it, were all from the shoulder up, the lack of nudes, and the image quality indicative of age.

He must have known what Elliott was thinking, too, because the few lights that were on in the living room were all turned down low.

"You want something to drink?" the liar asked him.

"Yeah. What you got?"

Elliott figured he'd at least get a drink out of it. If that didn't help, then he'd just have to make up something. Maybe let the guy suck on him for a while before he backed out because of the boyfriend who he suddenly didn't want to hurt. Yeah, he told himself, that excuse would work.

But he got a better look at his deceiver under the kitchen's bright light and saw he looked a little better from behind and was *kind of* thick in the one place he wanted him to be. Maybe a bit softer than he would have liked, though. Of course, if he kept pouring the vodka as freely as he was, it wasn't going to matter much anyway. With this late hour and enough liquor, just about everyone had some potential.

"Dat's good for me," Elliott told him.

"Sorry, I'm a little heavy-handed."

"I can see."

Elliott took the drink and threw a long sip of its liquid courage down his throat before he started up.

"I like your lil' shorts."

Elliott stuck his teeth out and stepped closer to see if he liked the way the shorts felt as much as he liked the way they looked. They fondled one another from the stark light of the kitchen back into the forgiving shadows of the living room that swallowed Elliott's dark skin whole. Sure enough, the urge in his pants returned and he unfastened his belt and released it.

139

GOODVIBESGUY removed his shirt and assisted Elliott with getting out of his, then yanking his jeans down to his ankles. He started with Elliott's nipples, letting his tongue tickle one as he stroked the other. Then he ventured south, dampening the furry strip below Elliott's navel as it led him to the next piece of male anatomy and when he found it, he welcomed it into his wide open mouth.

"Fuck, boy," Elliott moaned. "Mmmm . . ."

Making full use of the significant height advantage he had in this position, Elliott took hold of GOODVIBESGUY's chin and moved it upward, making him look him in the eye. Even in the near-darkness, Elliott could appreciate the face he had in his hands. Clear skin. Full lips. He liked his face.

So he pulled out and slapped it with his dick.

He taunted it, waving himself underneath GOODVIBES-GUY's nose. GOODVIBESGUY chased his dick in the dark, holding his mouth open and weaving around, eager to wrap his lips around it.

Finally done teasing, Elliott let him have it, all of it.

GOODVIBESGUY was being a little too polite, though, and Elliott needed him to know that he liked his dick serviced sloppily. He wanted deep-throat, gagging, bubbles of spit as GOODVIBESGUY sucked his dick. So, all at once, Elliott took him by the head and pushed down every last inch of himself. It wasn't as satisfying as he thought it would be for some reason. He couldn't put his finger on it, until he realized that his finger might have already been *in it.*

The palm of his hand was soiled.

"Um," he mumbled as he examined it. "I think I got some grease on my hand or something."

GOODVIBESGUY froze in horror as he ran his finger over his crown. When he saw the same soil over his fingers as Elliott had on his hand, he got up and ran, slamming shut what looked to be the bathroom door. Elliott stared into the slice of light sneaking out beneath the door for some explanation of what had sent the man who had just been on his knees having a good time into the bathroom hiding. The light from the kitchen helped him some, revealing an inky smear across the palm of his hand.

He had a good guess as to what it was.

"Hey, you . . .you good?" he asked the bathroom door.

"Can you just go?" the door answered.

"What's wrong? Don't worry 'bout—"

"Just go!" the door shot back.

"C'mon, bruh . . ." he pleaded. "You sho'?"

"Get the fuck out!" the door screamed.

Elliott could tell it meant every last word. It wanted him gone, now.

Even though he didn't understand why, he put his clothes back on and turned for the door he'd walked through just ten minutes ago. He knew the way out: down the stairs and a quick left would send him back out into the streets, free to do as he pleased with the rest of the night. And he knew just what he would do. It wouldn't be hard to find who he would be doing. But Elliott realized he was no longer in the mood to do so. Everything was always so easy with the men he met off the apps. He wasn't used to this kind of challenge, where there was a man who no longer wanted him but needed him, and for more than just his long dick.

And there was something about being needed in this new way that made him knock on the bathroom door. This surprised him because the situation in that bathroom was nothing simple, and simple was what he liked most when it came to his hookups, at least until now.

When the door violently swung open and GOODVIBES-GUY, with his fist clenched, yelled "Nigga, can you not fuckin' hear," Elliott didn't let it disturb him.

Instead, he answered calmly, not so unlike he'd do at the hospital when he had to care for an ornery patient. "I was just checking on you, yo'."

"I'm good. You can go."

"Yeah, yeah . . . I was just 'bout to," he said with every inclination to stop right there, except one. It was a ridiculous one, so ridiculous, in fact, that it just might work. "Can I see it?"

The watery-eyed man looked at him like he was dense. "Huh?"

"Yo' hair," answered Elliott. "Can I see it?"

"For what?" GOODVIBESGUY huffed.

Elliott could see that he was only making him more annoyed but the more he talked, the more chance he knew he had of breaking through. It was almost like that time Ms. Baker refused to eat breakfast and he'd sat with her and he'd sweet-talked her into finishing the whole plate. He swore he was the only one on hospital staff that could get through to that woman. And he approached this strange situation with a technique that was not unfamiliar to him.

"I used to cut my lil' brotha's hair sometimes."

"So what?" GOODVIBESGUY asked dryly.

"That mean I know a lil' somethin'." Elliott smirked when he said it. And even though he didn't receive a smirk back, he leaned a little closer through the door frame.

GOODVIBESGUY explained, "Look, I ain't tryna do nothin' no more tonight. Okay?"

"Okay. That's cool. I still wanna see, though."

"For what?"

"I'm the one that fucked yo' hair up. You could least lemme fix it."

He invited himself into the bathroom.

"I'on even know you like dat," he was reminded.

That was right. He only knew Elliott as bout2bustboi. *With a handle like that, what else was there to know?* Elliott asked himself. The username was simple, straight-to-the-point—things he *thought* he was.

And yet, here Elliott was, in some stranger's bathroom at God only knows o'clock, all but begging him to let his walls down, even though they were as high as his own would be on any other night.

"My name Elliott," he said, sharing with him who else he

was: a brother, a son, an uncle, a certified nursing assistant, a caretaker. Now it seemed a shame to him that he'd left all that out on his profile, and in person. All that had come over him earlier that had gotten him hot and bothered now seemed like a fever that had broken.

He was now speaking to him as Elliott, not bout2bustb0i.

"What yo' name is?" he asked.

"Justin."

Of course his name was Justin, Elliott thought. Friendly face. Big eyes. He looked like a Justin.

"Justin," he said. "Well, now ya know me."

"Whatchu want?" Justin asked plainly as he apprehensively held the towel wrapped around his waist.

Elliott ignored his trepidation. "What is it? That Redoo stuff?"

Justin nodded his head.

"Yeah, my barber use that shit on me sometimes. I told his ass to chill out wit' dat shit, but he still be sneakin' dat shit in. You know, they be trying to give you them fuckin' ruler-straight line-ups and shit. I just wash that shit right on out, though."

"Well, I got more to wash out than I got hair left."

Elliott saw that Justin's face had relaxed and a smile was now stretched across it. He was making an attempt at a joke. They were making progress.

"Gettin' old a muthafucka. Ain't it?"

"Yeah," Justin agreed.

Seeing how much Justin's face had relaxed, Elliott felt relaxed.

The sound of the shower running behind them was also relaxing, the water shooting out, hitting the tile and falling to the floor. He found a certain serenity to the pattern, so much so that the shower might as well have been a waterfall. He dared to think that Justin might have heard it the same.

"C'mon, let's wash dat shit out," Elliott said as he set himself free of his clothes.

He took Justin's hand and led him into the shower, unraveling his towel and letting it fall to the floor. Justin was clearly confused but he followed along.

Everything removed, they stepped in together. Under the water, the blackness came bleeding out from Justin's head and revealed to Elliott that the man he was sharing a shower with, the one that had advertised himself with a full head of hair, had a bald spot in the back of his head and that his hairline was fading in the front, too. But he could also see the thick pair of eyebrows planted on his face, which should also be known for its almond-like eyes and long, curly eyelashes. A face like that more than made up for what was missing just north of it, he thought.

Elliott rubbed his skinny fingers over the spot and massaged away Justin's fear into the water. And once it had gone down the drain, he kissed the bald spot and let his lips press against it until some of the ricocheting water got into his mouth. The splash across his face reminded him that he wasn't finished and there was so much more to discover in the nakedness of the man next to him. He explored Justin's body, finding some light stretch-marks on his hips, a birthmark on his inner thigh, some moles, a closed-up belly button piercing from forever ago, and a tiny scar on his knee. And he kissed and caressed them all before the steam from the shower overcame their vision of anything that lay outside this most immediate vicinity of one other.

CHAPTER 9
NIGHT DON'T NEED NO HELP

Justin left the barbershop bobbing to the beat of a song that played only in his freshly cut, goop-free head. As soon as he opened the door to his apartment, he turned his wireless speaker on and played the first thing that faintly resembled the melodic nature of this good mood he was in, Stevie Wonder's "For Once in My Life." Hips swaying, he whirled himself through every room in his one-bedroom, turning on every light. He praised Stevie Wonder inside the same bathroom where a man named Elliott, sweet, strange Elliott, had washed all the silliness out of his head.

He danced back into the living room, where his lip syncing turned to full-on shouting along to the joy coming out of the speaker and spreading all over the apartment he was blessed to rent all on his own. He felt the need to love on himself for that accomplishment and rolled onto the floor and wrapped his hands around his shoulders. He felt good in his own arms. He felt good all over, actually. And it felt good to feel good, so good he wanted to see it for himself. He held his phone above his face and let the camera show him the man who had been set free from hair and all of its imitations.

He was now completely bald. It felt entirely different than when he'd tried it before. Sure, it still made him look more like his father but this time he saw key differences in the early beginnings of the beard on his face. His father's beard was graying. His was just getting started. His father's beard was patchy. His connected. Having a beard was something new and something new, and natural, was exactly what he needed right now. Duke had said that he'd grow into it. It would just take some time.

But Justin wanted someone else to see this man that he saw glowing from recent grooming. The very first someone else that came to his mind was the very someone he had to thank for this liberation: Elliott.

He snapped a pic of himself and sent it to him along with a message.

New cut. You like?

He already knew the answer to this question because it had only been three nights earlier that Elliott had shown him affection when he'd had a liquid hairline. If he'd liked what he saw then, surely he would like what he saw now. But when Stevie's song was over, Justin was still lying on the rug and there was still no answer, yes or no, no text, no word at all from Elliott.

It was then that his depression emerged, crawling out from the corners of the apartment, latching onto his arms and holding him down on the floor. It rewrote the answer to Justin's question as he waited for yet another late response, another excuse about the crazy shifts Elliott worked at the hospital that were to blame, another night to pass since he had last seen him that one special time, another reason why he always felt so far away even though they lived so close. Feeling his mood changing by the minute, Justin picked himself up off the floor and got back into motion. He told himself that he looked too good to be stuck inside the house tonight and turned to social media for something to get into. He was reminded that Black Gay Pride was this weekend and before all the festivities officially kicked off, there were several events tonight to serve as their own sort of opening ceremony.

Justin scrolled through the promotional flyers, all of which featured greased-up models with sculpted abs, tight, tattooed

146

arms, and hair. His depression directed his thumb back to his text messages. When there was nothing new there, it told him everyone who was anyone was busy tonight getting Pride started. Elliott wasn't at work; he was out having a good time like everyone else was. He was too tied up getting ready to party to be texting the likes of Justin, some stranger with low self-esteem.

Justin felt the energy sapping out of him by the second and he fought to keep as much of it as he could. So he took a second look at the goings-on for tonight. One flyer stood out from all the club and party promotions because it was one he'd seen before: *Malicious Matters: Live.*

He rolled his eyes as he recalled his last run-in with Malcolm. That boy was beyond unbearable. But Justin had given him his word he would come to his show.

He thought to text his friend De'Leon to see if he would come with him but couldn't find the will to move his thumbs. Besides, once he got De'Leon involved, he was committed to going out and staying out and he wasn't sure how much endurance he had in him, if any at all.

Before he lost the last of his strength, Justin hurried and put his clothes back on. He walked out of the apartment so quickly, he hadn't even had the time to put a hat over his head. He paused and pressed his back against the door because he wasn't sure if he would need it or not. His depression slapped him on his bald head to come to his senses. It was Black Gay Pride. Everyone was going to being giving their best looks. What was he bringing besides that big, pill-shaped head of his?

His depression did him the favor of twisting the doorknob. All he had to do was open the door, go back and grab a hat to cover up the haircut he was convinced was so cute when it was really so fucking not. It was a fright. Duke could only do so much. There wasn't a barber in the world that could do anything to stop his ugliness from happening. And it was happening, one follicle at a time. On second thought, his depression concluded, it was probably best if he just stayed home tonight altogether. After all, if he didn't have any pride, why should he be at Pride? And besides, Pride was something for the pretty, young, up-and-coming gays. Justin was nearly thirty and every day of it showed on his big, wide face.

His hand slipped from the door handle and hung at his side. He wasn't going no-damn-where tonight.

If it made him feel any better he could walk down the hallway to try and fool himself that he was going out, but deep down, he knew where he'd end up. So just for the hell of it, he let himself pretend like he was actually going to partake in Black Gay Pride eve and took one small step down the hallway.

It was a stupid, indecisive, little step that hardly even made a sound.

Just to prove to himself how pathetic he was, he did it again to see if it was even possible that his next step would be weaker than his last. He could barely hear that footstep either.

It was like the floor didn't feel anything when he walked on it, didn't respect him enough to even adhere to physics and produce appropriate sounds in his presence. It must have been laughing at him right now.

He took another ridiculous step forward, this time with some intentional weight to it, so he could hear how flat even his best attempt fell. True, that one sounded more like a thud; but there had surely been better thuds across the old wooden floor. His sounded childlike in comparison, probably, as did the next one. He went down the hallway one slow and stupid step at a time, astonished at how absolutely pitiful he felt just being in motion. He felt sorry for himself, until he realized he'd made it to the stairs and that the door to his apartment was far behind him now, beyond his line of sight.

Now he was curious.

Just how far could he make it? How long would he last?

As a test, he let the weight of his defeated body lead him down the staircase.

Due to recent events, Chauncey didn't make the big fuss that he usually made about his birthday. This year, there was no daily post counting down each passing day until he turned twenty-five. There was also no birthday party. This year's celebration was simply a weekend stay at the host hotel for Black Gay Pride. With his work discount applied, it made for a more economical alternative than what he was accustomed to. Since he was in debt to Brontae for paying for his flight to LeMilion's funeral, he invited him to join out of gratitude.

It made no sense to Brontae, getting a hotel in the same city they lived in, but he went along anyway, figuring it might have been a little hard for Chauncey to have his first birthday without LeMilion, even if he didn't exactly show it.

"Aye!" Chauncey hollered, as he turned on the portable speaker.

He hopped on top of the hotel bed and began gyrating.

Seeing the futility in continuing to write, Brontae shut his laptop. He'd brought it in hopes he could sneak in some work on the beginnings of his first attempt at a novel. The rap song ratcheted up to a louder volume that made it clear that there would be no such thing happening this weekend.

I let him have the last word/
Make him think he really did something/
Then he shut tha fuck up/
When I throw dat pussy on him/
Yeah, yeah/
I throw dat pussy on him

Brontae sighed from the other double bed. "So, what's the plan tonight? Is Julius coming over too?"

"Julius?" Chauncey put a temporary freeze on his jubilation. "I ain't invite him."

"Why not?" asked Brontae.

149

"I mean . . . we cool but we ain't, like, *friends-friends*. No shade, but . . . I'on know him like dat. I'm just familiar with him," Chauncey answered coldly. "Besides, you know he got sticky fingas. Did you ever find your ear pods?"

Brontae shook his head at Chauncey. The past month had brought them closer together than they'd ever been before. They'd lost. They'd laughed. They'd mourned. And they had done it together, with Julius. But just when Brontae felt like he was getting to know him after five years of Friday nights, Chauncey had reverted to being the same as he'd always been—catty, unaffected, an asshole—and this time, Brontae got the feeling it was deliberate.

"You don't know me like dat either," said Brontae. "You still invited me. Or is that just because I paid—"

"So what? You, me and Julius supposed to be BFFs for life now just because . . ." Chauncey caught himself before mentioning anything or anyone that would kill his mood. "Whateva. If y'all so close, fine, tell him to come through but that's y'all friend, not mine, girl."

"Y'all?" Brontae repeated. "You mean me and LeMilion?" He emphasized LeMilion's name so Chauncey could remember Christian Memorial and the three-street town in the same way he remembered it. "Is that what you mean? Me and LeMili—"

"Brontae! Fuck! Lighten da fuck up! It's my birthday weekend. I'm tryna have some fun. I ain't tryna think 'bout all that."

"So that mean we can't even say his name now?"

"Fuck you," Chauncey said. He turned the music up even more and drowned out any further conversation.

Brontae regretted ruining his mood. Perhaps he had gone too far. As amends, he got up and poured them two shots from the several bottles of liquor they'd brought with them.

Chauncey accepted the apology in the form of the alcohol and downed it.

"So, seriously, what's the plan for tonight?" Brontae asked.

"I mean, it's early as fuck right now," Chauncey said as he adjusted the speaker's volume slightly. "We could pregame at the pool for a while before we go out. It should be poppin'. Then again, it's only Thursday. Everybody might still be checkin' in and shit, if they even here yet."

Chauncey's allergy to making firm plans annoyed Brontae to no end. He picked up his phone and began researching what was on the Black Gay Pride schedule for tonight.

"Oh, look. Malicious Matters is doin' a live show."

He showed Chauncey the flyer. "It's right here at the hotel, just downstairs."

"Ew." Chauncey scrunched up his face. "What I wanna see that ol' sloppy queen for? She funny?"

"Malicious Matters? He do a podcast I used to listen to. LeMilion used to like it t—"

"No thanks," Chauncey said with certainty. "But go if you want. We can meet up later. I'mma take a nap before it's time to go out, anyway. You better save some energy for tonight, bitch."

Thinking of all the energy that would be required to make it through the next three nights with the stranger he was sharing a double bedroom with, Brontae poured himself one more shot.

Malcolm stepped out to the front of the banquet hall and blew out his breath at the Black youth before him. This was for several reasons. First, he was hot and felt like the AC was blowing right past him, if it was blowing at all. Second, there were only about thirty-something people in attendance when there should have been at least seventy-something, according to online RSVPs. After months and months of Internet networking, posting, reposting and follow-for-follows, he still couldn't get the Black gays to show up to support one of their own and that was a shame. Third, he was nervous. Being here in person was nothing like being behind a mic recording from home. When he looked out into the few rows of seats that weren't empty, he saw an expectation for nothing less than thorough entertainment in the eyes of the gays that sat with their arms folded and their phones charged and capable of capturing him at any time, at any angle.

But way in the back, farther out from where everyone else was seated, Malcolm also saw a bloody-faced figure that was looking, no, waiting, for him to do something else from the platform he stood on. It was Kameron—that poor waiter from the diner—just as he'd left him, with a hurting all over his face.

This figment of his imagination was not new. Ever since that night at the diner, Kameron had been in dreams that had disturbed his sleep, at the back of his guilt-ridden mind, and now he was here haunting him before the show even got started. His spiritual presence elicited a sigh from Malcolm before he spoke into the mic.

"Heeeeeey, whores! Heeeey!" Malcolm started up.

And so did the audience.

"What's the tea, bitch?" they yelled back.

Now that they were speaking the same language, Malcolm had to match their energy and since their energy was charged, Malcolm would have to forget about his fear and the lone spirit sitting in the shadows of the room. He had to give them who they came to see—the him that wasn't him.

"Happy Pride, whores!"

Malcolm gave them a moment to bask at his grand arrival, to get a good look at the fashion being brought to them tonight in all-black: skintight jeans, an oversized hoodie, and a pair of those clunky sneakers everyone was wearing nowadays.

"Where my bottoms at? Y'all ready to get Pride weekend muthafuckin' started? Y'all left all y'all troubles and flushed 'em down the toilet too? Just wanna make sure the girls are prepared, ya know," he joked.

The bottoms howled to let him know that they were here and most definitely ready.

"Ooooh! Y'all naaaaaasty," he teased.

Next, he took a roll call for the tops in attendance, but of the maybe twelve that responded, he only counted two.

"No! I'm talkin' 'bout true tops! Cuz you know some of you just use your peen on a part-time basis."

Brontae filled one of the many vacant seats available. He had come to the show to get a break from Chauncey more than anything. Once an avid listener of the *Malicious Matters* podcast, tonight Brontae found himself rolling his eyes at Malcolm, off-put and even bored. But the rest of the audience was eating up his every word. Once Malcolm got them amped up and hollering, he moved on to the first segment of the show, "Messy Matters," which involved his commentary on trending topics in pop culture.

The first item of discussion was an easy one. Just about everyone who watched *Hot Mess: Atlanta* collectively agreed that Nola Washington never should have told that big-mouth Samara that she was pregnant if she knew Lil Vengeance was going to make her have an abortion. Now everybody on the show knew all her business and was looking for a baby bump that would never show. And that didn't even include the blogs that were running with the story and making her look all kinds of foolish. But when the topic came up, Malcolm was a little light on words.

"Neva trust a bitch with tattooed eyebrows," was all he had to say on the subject. He couldn't find it in him to care enough to give his opinion on a show that was just that: *a show.* It was nothing but D-list celebrities pretending like they weren't following some stupid script, performing countless takes in front of cameras, only for it to be carefully edited into televised entertainment. Bored as he realized he was with it, he struggled to even call it that. But it was so popular. This was what *they* watched, what *they* cared about. And so did he, didn't he?

Malcolm wasn't so sure anymore.

He moved on to something he was more certain of: Aura Era and her third time checking out of rehab in only two days.

"Oh, Aura Era," he sighed. " Girl, where the fuck do I even begin?"

The audience braced themselves for what they knew would be Malicious at his best, ranting on and on with the worst things that were left to say about the disgraced diva. Malcolm was about to give it to them, but then he noticed Justin enter the room like he owed it an apology, looking lost even after he'd found a seat. He was late too but he was here, just as he promised he would be. But his "hair" wasn't. Even Justin had changed, Malcolm thought, and change looked good on him. Malcolm wondered if Justin knew it, though—but then he remembered that he had to find something new to say about Aura Era, and fast.

"A mess. Sis just out here ghosting sobriety and shit."

Malcolm made it through the rest of the segment with fading momentum, uninterested in anything he was saying, unsure as to what was coming over him and unable to not see the judgmental look on Kameron's imaginary face beneath all the gore.

"Okay, so the next part of the show, for those of you not familiar, is called 'LGBTQ . . . and A.' So, this where you get to ask me anything and I gotta give my big, gay-ass answer. Any questions?"

The transition to the next segment picked up some of the enthusiasm the audience had lost and a few hands went up. Brontae had been watching the whole show in wonderment and had questions about what exactly he was witnessing. A meltdown, maybe? Or just a mediocre show? He had just enough liquid courage in him to find out directly which one it was and almost raised his hand. But others were more willing to seize this opportunity to speak, to put on the show that Malicious Matters had failed to. So it was the loudest and liveliest that stood out, the ones flopping their arms in the air.

"Mmmm . . . bitch, I got something to say," said a voice that needed no microphone to be heard.

Malcolm pretended like there were better candidates he could call on and looked past the man bursting to be in control of the room, if only temporarily. But gracefully Malcolm relinquished his authority and pointed at the man with the high cheekbones and lips curled with confidence in whatever was about to come out of them. Malcolm's cousin Arnaud came down the aisle and, after some configurations, gave the man a microphone. He was all too happy to spill his story.

"Okay, so I gotta dude, right? Ya know, we kick it. Been doin' it for a lil' minute now. Sex slappin'. All of dat. Ya know . . ."

He popped his gums to emphasize his point as the room waited in anticipation of his punch line.

"So basically, he cool and all or whateva. But, um . . . Dude ain't circumcised."

He gave the room a moment to gasp at this revelation.

"No, ma'am! Uh uh!" the room said in mock shock.

"Yes, he's as uncut as the cake at a Jehovah Witness birthday party. Like, I tried but it just taste so salty. Like, yuck! I can't be puttin' no burrito in my damn mouth when I would much rather a banana. Feel me? So Malicious, tell me, what a bitch s'posed to do?" he asked in exaggerated desperation.

"Break up with dat nigga!" "That's nasty," the room advised.

Seeing the seriousness on their faces as they called for the immediate disintegration of the entire relationship because of something as simple and natural as skin made Malcolm sick in a way he hadn't been sick before. They were vicious, unforgiving, and downright mean, just like the comments they'd left on *his* videos, *his* posts, *his* content that was meant to be vicious, unforgiving, and downright mean. But witnessing what he'd put out into the universe come back to him in such physical form, living and breathing and Black and gay and ignorant, was too much and too loud for Malcolm to ignore.

He gripped the mic with intention and addressed them.

"Baby, let me tell you something . . . Maybe if you're fortunate enough to find somebody in this fucked-up ass world, maybe you should be so busy getting down on your knees every night thanking God for sending you someone to come home to after being out in this crazy-ass shit all day that there never would come a night where you be ungrateful enough to come here and complain to a room of unfamiliar, unhappy queens about *your man*, which, by the way, most of them would go behind your back to gladly snatch and slurp up what you don't want to. Myself included."

The room wasn't ready for the truth that had trespassed into the banquet hall. It took a few seconds that felt like minutes, long and uncomfortable minutes, for everyone to figure out how to respond to it. It seemed to take even longer for Malcolm. He wasn't sure how the words, so many words, had come out of his mouth. It didn't sound like something he'd say, but he knew that he had said it. He also didn't know what would happen next.

The looks on everyone's faces all read shock. He couldn't clearly make out what he saw in the spirit of Kameron sitting all the way in the back, whether it was a smile or surprise.

"Well, damn. That was some shade right there!" someone said.

"Ooh . . . the shade of it all," said someone else as he pointed his phone's camera at the stunned man who had asked a question and gotten "read for filth," as everyone was putting it.

The room went into an uproar, raucously repeating the same sentiments.

So that's what it was, Malcolm gathered. They'd all heard what he'd said and decided to deem it shade. Not just shade but grade-A shade, a masterpiece of a monologue from someone that had a true talent at throwing it.

Somewhere deep inside him, Malcolm knew that shade shouldn't be thrown when it was dark out because the night didn't need the help. It brought more than enough darkness with it all on its own. And although there was a part of him that was tempted to tell them all just that, he let it be.

Everyone's phones and attention were on him. And very soon, if not already, he would be on the Internet. Since he knew his way around that place better than he knew his way out of this awkward position his mouth had put him in, he laughed and let them turn his words into what they expected out of him, what entertained them, what would make him into a meme, and what would eventually, in its Internet existence, go on to get him many more followers.

Malcolm would go on to do more shows too. And just like this one, there would always be someone, somewhere in the audience who he knew was watching him differently than the rest and waiting, needing him to be better than he was.

While everyone left the show hugging onto their phones, eagerly responding to texts about what time and what place to meet, what to wear and where to go, when Justin turned his phone over in his hand, it was naked of notifications.

That was exactly why he was glad he'd decided to come to the show after all. Even if he didn't find anything funny in what Malcolm had said, it had taken his mind off of Elliott for a little over an hour. Hoping to kill more time, Justin wandered over to the hotel's bar and found a seat.

"Hey, you know him?" the man sitting next to him asked. "Malicious Matters?"

"Oh, Malcolm?" Justin replied.

"Yeah, I saw you talking to him after the show."

"Just saying hello really. We used to work together. That's all," Justin said with a dry tone that he hoped would disassociate him from Malcolm as much as possible.

But Justin could tell from the way he was biting his lips that his barstool neighbor was bothered and needed to say something.

"So, what was that?" he asked. "I was sitting in there like 'what the fuck?'"

"As was I," Justin said, relieved to share his opinion with someone who had seen the same thing he had seen.

"Yeah, I used to listen to his show and I ain't never seen him act like that."

"Used to?" Justin asked, curious at the choice of tense.

His friendly neighbor was happy to elaborate.

"Yeah, used to. Sometimes, when I was bored at work."

"Why'd you stop? You not bored at work no more?"

Justin's flirtiness surprised him. He wasn't even sure he was attracted to (or sexually compatible with) the man who had sparked this conversation. Plus, the man was obviously younger than him by at least a year or two.

"Oh no, I am. All the time actually," he said, flirting back.

157

Suddenly Justin didn't feel so foolish.

"Then why'd you stop?"

"Well," he started before immediately stopping to take a deep breath. "I guess what I used to find funny, ain't no more. Does that make sense?"

"Actually, that makes all the sense in the world to me," Justin said, suddenly aware of how comfortable he felt talking to this perfect stranger who looked him in his eyes when he talked, unimpressed and uninterested in anything besides the next thing he had to say. If Justin was wearing an orange jumpsuit, he wasn't sure he would have even noticed it.

His attention was solely on the conversation. So Justin didn't think about the jeans he wished he had worn instead tonight or the hat he had thought to put on. He didn't think at all. He just talked as the stranger he was seated next to listened like it was the last thing he would ever hear.

"So, are you here for Black Gay Pride?" he asked Justin after they'd given their scathing review of *Malicious Matters: Live* in its entirety.

"Oh no. I'm not staying at the hotel. I live here in the city. I just came here to see the show. What 'bout you?"

"I'm staying at the hotel but I live here too, actually. I'm just here for a friend's birthday, so it's a birthday and Black Gay Pride situation."

"Well, sounds like you got a wild weekend ahead," Justin said, backing off at the mention of this "friend."

"Not that kinda friend. I mean, like, actual friend," he said as if on cue.

Justin turned and got a better look at the man bold enough to be inside his head. He saw the brown in his face more clearly and came to appreciate how much its dull shade suited him with his understated features—a nose that was neither big or small, plain and perfect lips, and dark-rimmed glasses that slightly hid the attractiveness all of his average parts somehow added up to.

"I'm Justin," he offered.

"Brontae."

Brontae had a puppy named Tea Cake and a recently deceased friend named LeMilion. The name was pronounced *lee-mill-e-on*. And Brontae, poor thing, was still broken up about losing LeMilion. Justin knew all of these things because he had been at the bar with Brontae talking for nearly an hour now. They'd covered a lot in that short time: Justin starting culinary school in the fall, Brontae transitioning from screenwriting to starting the novel he'd come to find out he'd always wanted to write, their shared lack of enthusiasm for Black Gay Pride weekend, and even a little bit of Greek mythology. All their talking, whether it was about something or nothing much at all, had done them both good.

"So, what's your deal? You dating somebody?" Brontae asked, emboldened by the fourth drink Justin could account for at least.

His phone dinged before he could answer. It was a series of dings, actually, so many that both Justin and Brontae glanced at the screen.

It was Elliott. Whenever Elliott did get around to replying, he usually did it all at once in a burst of blue bubbles. The timing of his response, whatever it read, was too awkward for Justin to allow himself the exhalation he'd been waiting for so he swallowed it for now.

"Oh, well, there go my answer," Brontae quipped.

Justin finished the last of his drink, hoping that by the time he put the glass down, he'd know how to explain that there was a man he had just met the other night and how that night, as recent as it was, had helped him in a whole other way than this one had. He couldn't lie. That night had happened and its magic deserved to be mentioned.

"I dunno . . . He just a guy I met the other night, to be honest," Justin tried to explain, unashamed of the smile that came across his face.

"Uh oh. That's not good for me at all."

"It's nothin' like dat."

"If it was nothing then you wouldn'ta told me the truth," Brontae pointed out. "You could have easily lied about it and you didn't. Let me guess. You met him on the app."

Justin tensed up a little at the accuracy of Brontae's words.

"Yeah, basically but that don't mean we dating."

Brontae took another drink. His eyes dimmed a little after the murky liquid went into his mouth.

"No, it definitely don't," he said, staring off. With his eyes focused someplace Justin couldn't see but could feel, Brontae asked, "Do you ever get tired of it?"

"The app?" asked Justin.

"The app, all of the apps, the pics, the profiles, the looking, all the hims and hes we meet at night that we never seem to know enough about . . . all of it."

There was a big fat *yes* that Justin should have said, would've said, but the relief in hearing someone else say out loud everything he'd felt was something he had to enjoy in silence.

"Ya know, I don't know a single gay guy in a relationship right now? Like, an actual, long-term relationship. Not a open relationship or nothing. I'm talkin' about just two gay guys that are actually together. Nothin' on the side. No slippin' or dippin' out. Just, like, united and . . . happily together and shit. Do you?"

"Well, my friend Desmond and his boyfriend have been together for some time . . ." Justin thought for a second. "Come to think of it, I saw one of them online the other day so never mind."

Brontae snapped out of his gaze to join Justin in a laugh and then he started a new path on this branching subject with the most earnest expression in his drunk eyes.

"Look, Justin, I won't waste your time. I haven't had a conversation with someone like I'm having with you in a long time and I don't think you have either, if I had to guess, at least. I'm not asking you to be my boyfriend right here and right now, but I'm just sayin' that . . . I'm just sayin' I'm . . . not scared to see you when the day after this night comes."

It was the sweetest thing of all things any man had ever said to Justin. And Brontae hadn't blinked once when he'd said any of it. Life looked so much easier for Justin—until Brontae decided to attach just two more words.

"Unlike Elliott."

The casual way he said it rubbed Justin raw.

Brontae leaned close to Justin's face, his breath bitter of alcohol and stinking of cigarette smoke, confident he could lean even closer, if he liked. He looked just above Justin's eyes and smirked as he slid his unfamiliar fingers behind Justin's head and across his bare scalp.

Depression didn't let Justin stop him. It told Justin that an undeserving ugly like him should be thankful for this affection he was lucky to get, twice this week at that. But then Justin realized that it wasn't his depression that he was hearing. It was Brontae. And he was saying it with two words and one stroke of his hand.

"You don't know anything about him," Justin said defensively.

"Yeah, you don't either, I bet," Brontae said, as if he was giving a helpful warning.

Justin wiped Brontae's touch off his head like it was germs. He realized that he wouldn't stop with that either. He would have to let him know that he had touched something he wasn't supposed to touch. That even if he was lonely and probably a good writer and had a dead friend and a way with words, he couldn't let him touch him like *that*. And that if it weren't for Elliott, the place he had just untenderly touched him might not be what it was now. And he liked to think that it was better. Bald but better.

Even if it turned out Elliott was the worst of the worst, he couldn't let some stranger spoil the good he had gotten out of a night he might not ever get again. Even if he didn't have hair, he had hope and if Brontae wasn't careful, he was going to lose his.

"You right. Maybe we don't know enough about these hims and hes we meet at night. Then again . . . maybe we know just as much as we need to make it through to the next night," Justin said, realizing that his words weren't just for Brontae—they were for himself, too.

"That's deep. That's real . . . deep," said Brontae, before he offered to get Justin another drink.

Justin was briefly tempted to take him up on it. One more drink and he might have been able to forget what Brontae had just said and done and meet him on his level of drunkenness. But he knew his tolerance well enough to know that he was already on the brink of feeling how Brontae felt—drunk and despaired—and he didn't want to come any closer to it than he already was. So, to keep his night with Brontae as special as it had been, Justin knew that he would have to end it here.

"No, I'm good . . . I think I'm gonna get out of here."

"You leaving?" Brontae asked, visibly confused. "Damn, I hope I didn't—"

"Don't worry about it," Justin replied, getting up from the barstool.

He thanked Brontae for the drinks and conversation and gave him a wholehearted hug, getting all the warmth he needed for the night from Brontae and returning it. When Brontae asked him for his number and handed him his phone to enter it, Justin reached it back to him, choosing to grab a pen from the bar and write his number down on a napkin instead.

"Well, damn, alright then," Brontae said. "Old school."

Justin smiled and slid the napkin to Brontae. Then he left him at the bar, to watch the back of his bald head with the new growth Justin was only now aware of.

CHAPTER 10

THE MASC BOTTOM IN THE MIRROR

Chauncey had always had a thing for hotels. Ever since he was a kid, there was something about sharing the most temporary of housing with total strangers that allured him. Being the hospitality aficionado that he was, he always thoroughly inspected the amenities each hotel had to offer. That was another thing he liked about hotels. They all had something to offer, even ones like this one that was less than luxurious compared to the hotel he worked in.

Of course, it could be said that just staying in the host hotel for Black Gay Pride, in the thick of all the action and out-of-towners checking in and out, was the greatest perk of all. In fact, that was one of the main reasons he'd booked a room. But Chauncey wasn't satisfied with just that perk, so he had to test the water pressure in the shower to see if it was strong. He had to review the room service menu in case there was some specialty item on it like seafood spaghetti. He had to turn the air down to the lowest temperature possible to make sure the AC wasn't lazy and worked like it should. Then he played around with the lamps and lights to see what creative freedom he had in regards to lighting schemes. Surprisingly, he had quite a bit: soft, recessed lighting; a dimmer; bar lights on both sides of the vanity. He was glad he'd taken the effort to find the best feature the hotel's website had foolishly left off.

He settled on a lighting scheme that looked romantic and warm in all the right places, and if it wasn't for the two beds, he might have forgotten he was sharing the room with Brontae.

He figured he still had plenty of time before Brontae made it back, so he decided he'd use it to do what he always did when he lucked up with a room with good lighting: update his nudes.

He put on a song that made him feel sexy, Vanessa Lovechild's "Beat My Box," and he made himself a drink. Then he stripped out of his clothes and approached the full-length mirror. In this light, his lips looked as pink as grapefruit and every ab in his six-pack glistened like gold.

He turned to the side a little and tested his angles, which side made his ass look bigger and which hand to hold the phone with in case he wanted to keep his dick out of the shot.

After snapping exactly one pic that he already didn't like, his phone sounded.

It was a notification from MENAFTER10.

He opened the app. It was immediately clear to him that the app was running on Black Gay Pride time now and it showed in the hyperactivity on MENAFTER10. There was a lot happening and it was all happening fast. There were now 913 unread messages sitting in his inbox. Twelve of them had come within the past twenty minutes, probably while he was down the hall getting ice or maybe while he was downstairs taking pics of the pool. There were so many messages and so many men who were all so very near. Judging from the unusually convenient distances he saw online, he didn't think he'd have to go further than the elevator to meet anyone.

Chauncey popped open the profile of who looked to be the cutest of the twelve senders.

He might have also been the youngest, Chauncey realized upon closer inspection. He was even younger than Chauncey was and by several years. Normally, this posed no problem but seeing as how he was just a couple hours from turning twenty-five, he hesitated.

Funny, he had to admit, though he was just shy of being

twenty-five, he felt like he'd been doing this same thing, playing this same game online, for so much longer. Trading pics. Flipping through profiles. Weeding through man after man, only to still be single.

Still, no matter how tiring it was, he had enough energy tonight to take the twenty-one-year-old dick yungyellowboi was advertising and he quickly replied to his message before he could give it any further thought; and to speed things up, he went ahead and unlocked his profile for him too.

Then he returned his attention to his reflection in the mirror and let it remind him of all that he had to offer.

It put him in a generous mood and he decided to go back through his recent unread messages and bless a couple more people with a reply, with the privilege of his open profile. He was more generous in who he selected, too. He was coming up on that particular time of night when being a good fuck mattered more than being good-looking.

That ungodly hour was approaching fast.

Too fast for yungyellowboi apparently, as he had yet to respond.

Being too impatient to wait for him, Chauncey went with the first person who did respond.

D'Sagitarrius: *u know u sexy af right?*

The compliment put a smile on Chauncey's face. Being sexy was the best thing to be during Black Gay Pride. Every gay here either wanted to fuck him or be him. They didn't care if he didn't have a well-paying job. They didn't care about his regrets. They only cared about the one thing he knew he always delivered on—his looks. It felt good to be reminded of why he never missed this annual celebration.

Chauncey took another sip of his drink and fell onto the bed, stretching his naked body across it as he held his phone up to the ceiling.

Several other replies came back; even yungyellowboi

responded eventually, but they had all come too late. Chauncey had already settled on D'Sagitarrius and it wasn't because he was the prettiest or had the best body or looked like his dick swung the lowest. It was because he talked like he did. The speed at which he messaged Chauncey back certainly helped too. Chauncey liked that. He also liked his command over their conversation, which he kept active and engaging.

> D'Sagitarrius: *so u gonna let me make dat ass mine?*
> redNready69: *unlock ur profile and well see*

A winky face went along with the request.

D'Sagitarrius fully revealed himself to be a strapping, broad-shouldered man with skin that was so dark it seemed to go beyond being just brown. He was *black-Black* and built like someone that had been in shape once, with his chest and arms loosely holding onto a previously athletic form. His dick was more girthy than lengthy. It was also ashy and uncut. That was all fine with Chauncey because, once the hardness formed between his legs, it was no longer about what he liked and disliked, it was about what he wanted, and how soon he could get it. And right now, he wanted to get his birthday weekend started with some decent dick inside him.

> redNready69: *wanna come over? I'm at Hotel Moore*
> D'Sagitarrius: *fasho. I'm close by*
> D'Sagitarrius: *send me anothr pic of that pretty ass*

Running low on nudes, Chauncey took a second look at his most recent pic, the one that he'd taken just minutes ago. He still didn't like it but sent it anyway, certain that it would satisfy D'Sagitarrius.

> D'Sagitarrius: *mmmmm*
> D'Sagitarrius: *I'm tryna spell my name in that shit 2nite*
> D'Sagitarrius: *so wassup? You got the room 2 urself ritght?*

redNready69: *Yeah*

D'Sagitarrius: *perfect. So let me come fuck dat pretty ass in a ugly way then*

Provoked by his language, Chauncey touched himself with his free hand.

redNready69: *cum thru then nigga*

D'Sagitarrius: *aight. but just so u know, this might hurt a bit my nigga*

Chauncey bit his lip at the challenge.

redNready69: *I can handle a lil hurting*

redNready69: *but my bday is literaly in a couple hours so don't go too hard on me lol*

D'Sagitarrius: *oOh really??!! So the birthday boi want me to beat it up huh?*

D'Sagitarrius: *das cool. u can start ur birthday wit me inside u*

redNready69: *dat would be hot*

D'Sagitarrius: *well shit. Im ready when u are.*

redNready69: *ok I'll hit u up in a bit.*

Chauncey took his hand off himself and sat up in the bed. The clock was on.

There were so many men coming into town for the weekend's festivities. He and D'Sagitarrius would have to hurry to meet and do everything they'd just said they'd do to each other before one, if not both of them, went and did it to someone else instead.

So Chauncey went to work. Feeling a slight uneasiness in the pit of his stomach from the shawarma he'd eaten with Brontae earlier, he started his preparation by opening up the new pack of saline enemas he'd brought with him. He went into the bathroom, which was lit so strongly he looked washed out by all its whiteness: the cream-painted walls, the clinical-looking ceramic tiled floor, the ivory sink basin. Everything in the room that wasn't white was silver—the shower rod, the sink, the frame around the big mirror that almost took up an entire wall on its own.

It was so big, it made Chauncey look at himself just once more. This time, though, he wasn't studying how flat his stomach was or the gains in his biceps. He was looking at the man, the "masc bottom" as he described himself on his MENAFTER10 profile, and how ready he was for all that was about to happen to him tonight, this weekend, and beyond.

He looked as ready as he was ever going to be.

Snapping out of reflection, Chauncey went to the toilet and took the baby blue, translucent plastic enema out of its wrapper. He squatted over the seat and eased its white, pointed tip into his anus, squeezing the room-temperature, saline solution up his rectum. After crushing the enema pump in the palm of his hand, the solution spilled back out of him along with shapeless bits of stool.

This was merely a warm-up.

He stood up, poured the remaining solution into the toilet and hobbled over to the sink, refilling the pump with warm water, then screwing the tip back on.

Now began the real routine.

Chauncey was so familiar with the process of self-induced shitting that when the water went jetting up into him it didn't hurt. When his body reacted to the heated liquid that had been shot up into it by violently erupting fragmented excretion into the toilet water, Chauncey hardly even flinched. He got up from the toilet once more, his asshole slick and sensitive from the quaking excess of excretion that had just passed through it, and flushed the brownish, watery mess down the bowl. He returned to the faucet and repeated the process over and over, purging himself of all of his shit and, oddly, enjoying it. In fact, Chauncey occasionally administered the enemas on his off-nights from being a masc bottom on MENAFTER10. Sometimes, the water he replaced into the plastic pump wasn't just warm. Sometimes, he ran the water a little hot, so it burned when it ran up the walls of his anal cavity.

Sometimes, Chauncey needed to feel the burn to feel anything at all.

"Shit," he cried out as the last bottle of water went to work up his rectum. He'd run the water too hot again.

It took a full two minutes of squirming in discomfort for him to recover. Once he did, he told himself it was an accident, denying the pleasure he got out of this pain. He made up for it by filling the next round with cold water. He went on repeating until there was less and less to flush down the toilet, no brown, no solids. It took a while before he was satisfied enough with his cleanliness to stop and throw the dented-up pump in the trash. Exactly how much time it had taken, he wasn't sure of. He thought to check and see. He opened the bathroom door, releasing the odor of watered-down defecation, and went into the bedroom for his phone.

"Fuck," he said, looking at the time.

It was 10:12. He had lost a whole hour pushing an enema up his ass, too consumed with being clean. He wasn't the only person mad at himself for letting that happen.

The phone was filled with messages and all of them were from D'Sagitarrius, each one more impatient than the last. Chauncey quickly put together an apology.

I'm sooooooo sorry.
was in the bathroom getting ready
hopping in the shower now

Finally, after spending roughly thirty seconds refreshing the app, checking for replies, Chauncey got word back from D'Sagitarrius. Actually, it wasn't even a word. It was only one letter.

K

It was the most unfriendly letter of the entire alphabet. And when used on MENAFTER10, it was especially rude.

But Chauncey deserved it, so he took the single-letter slap in the face without complaint. He would need to do more to make up for losing track of time. Back in the bathroom, he got the shower started, and turned on his photography skills, jamming his phone between the faucet handle and spout so that it stayed in place. He checked to be sure the camera pointed directly at the shower, mentally measuring how close he'd need to zoom it in and where he'd need to stand to get a shot of his wet ass that was so sexy, D'Sagittarius would forget all about that one hour he'd wasted waiting.

First, he needed to wash off from all the douching he'd done. So he went into the shower. Not wanting to risk getting any remnants that may have splashed onto his cheeks on the white towel, he used his bare hands to wash off his bottom. It was while he had the soap lathered in his hand as he stuck it between himself that he felt a light fuzziness in the crack of his behind. It wasn't much but being "the baddest masc bottom you'll ever meet," as his MENAFTER10 profile put it, he thought to run a razor over that ass right quick to keep his reputation intact.

Chauncey reached for a towel off the rack and wrapped it around his waist as he ran back out into the bedroom dripping wet. He pulled his suitcase from the closet and opened the small pouch on the side, removing a bag of disposable razors. He took one and hurried back into the bathroom. His phone dinged as soon as he shut the door. His hand still wet, he picked the phone up and read the message from D'Sagittarius.

Waiting...

Hastily, Chauncey put the phone back in place, slung the towel onto the counter and went back into the shower, under the stream of warm water. He lathered the soap over his behind again and took the plastic razor across his flesh, dragging it carefully over the wet skin and white suds of soap. Then, he turned the razor at an angle, slowly scraping the blade into the crevice of his behind. When he finished, he rinsed the razor off and set it on the shower's soap dish. He slid the shower door open, looking at the phone that was propped up with its eye on him.

He got out of the shower again, realizing that because the shower door had been open, some water was spraying onto the tiled floor of the bathroom. He took the discarded towel off the bathroom counter and laid it across the floor to soak up some of the ricocheting water. Then he picked the phone back up and started the timer on the camera.

All set, he rushed back into the shower. Turning his back to the camera with a slight arch so that his ass looked as enticing as possible, he held his legs tight so that his thighs rubbed together and only the water ran between them.

He held this pose until the camera flashed.

Immediately, he hopped out again and grabbed the phone to review his work. It wasn't his best. It was a little blurry, even, but his ass came out clear enough and it looked just fine.

He slapped a few filters over the pic, threw some fast edits on top of it and hit *Send*.

almost ready 4 u

He was just setting his foot back in the shower when he got a reply.

a lil blurry
take it again
so I can see wat dat ass look like before i come wreck it

It was the least he could do, Chauncey supposed, and he obliged his request once more.

yeah one sec

Chauncey reset the camera's timer and went back into the shower, intent on taking his greatest nude yet. After the camera flashed, he snapped out of his pose and stepped out the shower, one foot at a time. The first foot landed on the damp towel he was using as a bathroom mat but the other foot missed this target and hit the tile floor, then went sliding on the water-slicked surface. In this one mistaken movement, Chauncey lost his balance and collapsed. Gravity took him down in an instant. His backside slammed onto the floor, his lower half outside the shower, his upper half inside.

The back of his head hit the porcelain flooring hard. The thud of the impact echoed in his dizzy consciousness as the pain struck him all at once and the water from the shower crashed onto his face. He remained immobile as the pain circulated in concentrated waves from across the center of his head to his neck to the small of his back. His fall played over and over in a loud loop that banged in his brain as the pain spread. The sound of his phone, a new message alert, was even more painful to hear but the familiar buzz helped his mind recover.

Then he remembered how he had fallen in the first place and why the phone was on the floor outside the shower and not propped up on the counter as he'd recalled leaving it.

He had stretched his arm all the way out to get the phone as he was getting out the shower and slipped. He'd done it so naturally, he hadn't even remembered doing it. That was how it had happened and he had done it all to himself. Slowly, he attempted to move, lifting his legs and bringing his knees to his torso. He curled his upper half and sat himself up as the shower continued pouring down on top of his head. He gave himself a full minute before trying to stand, supporting himself against the shower door and wall. Cautiously, he limped out of the shower.

Seeing the phone on the bathroom floor, he kneeled over and grabbed it, thinking that he might have to use it to call for help.

Before he did, he inspected his body for any sign of injury. As sore as his head felt, he didn't feel any bumps. There was a scuff at the bottom of his back but from what he could see in the mirror, it was minor. Perhaps he wouldn't need to call for help, he figured, and placed the phone down. But when he did, he noticed a small smear of blood across the screen. He reexamined his body in search of the source. It wasn't coming from his head. There wasn't blood anywhere on him, as far as the mirror could tell. On the floor though, he found a few crimson droplets, the closest of which was centered right between his feet.

It took him a moment to realize that the blood was seeping from his behind. It took even longer to realize that this blood wasn't from the fall but from the razor he'd rushed and run across his self just minutes ago. His fingertips were coated in it too, he discovered.

The phone dinged again and before Chauncey knew it, he had picked it up and held it in his blood-stained hands.

There were two new messages from D'Sagitarrius.

whats the hold up???
HELLO???!!!

Reading the messages with the tint of blood over the screen made Chauncey tighten his grip on the phone. Thinking of D'Sagitarrius impatiently waiting for a preview of the ass that was currently bleeding onto the bathroom floor in polite drips and drops made it even tighter. The darkness he saw in the red smidge glossed over the app made his whole body tremble as a truth came to him.

He'd met a lot of men, done a lot and ignored a lot. There was a possibility he might very well have that same thing LeMilion had. This thought was not new but he'd never allowed himself to fully see it for what it was. When the thought tried to undress itself, he'd always covered it up before it could. Now, though, he could see it in its nakedness as well as he could see his own in the mirror. Even if he did have *it*, it wasn't the possibility of dying that scared him. It was the trying. Trying to take better care of himself. Trying to make better choices for himself. Trying to tell his truth to men that only knew how to lie. Trying not to end up in Christian Memorial Hospital, in a room with no flowers, no balloons.

He looked at his face closely in the mirror as a tear trickled down his nose. It wasn't fair to compare himself to LeMilion, even if he did have *it*. He knew other people who were positive and they were all very much alive. Chances were he'd be more like them than like LeMilion. But, then again, he thought, LeMilion had died alone, buried in judgment for how he'd lived his life. How far off was Chauncey from that, really? Was he not alone now, even in his time of need?

No, he told himself. His mother actually loved him. He could call her. He loosened his hold on the phone as he considered explaining to his dear mother how he had hurt himself preparing to meet some man in some hotel at some hour of the night she wasn't familiar with. That wasn't an option. Once he realized it, his hand tightened around the phone once more.

Then he realized something else too. Deep down in his heart, LeMilion's death had left him feeling more burdened than bereaved. It had made him see that the world was a sick, sad place and sex was as important to it as the sun. The problems he saw in the world now partly included him. But what was he supposed to do about it? He couldn't change the way things were. He could only change himself.

He considered an easier reality he could live with. After all, there was an alternative to all of this. Maybe he didn't have *it*. Maybe the God he prayed to spared him just one more time and he wasn't HIV-positive. What then, though? He couldn't just go on as he was because it would be stupid to see what had happened to LeMilion and still behave the only way he knew how to behave. He wasn't stupid. Was he?

He was going to have to do better because now he knew better. He saw that fact clearly in the mirror. And he would do better, or so he wanted to believe. There was a lot he wanted to believe about himself though. All he knew for certain was that he could no longer do what he was doing, in good conscience.

So why in the hell am I doing it then? he asked the man or masc bottom or whoever the hell it was standing in the mirror crying.

174

When he couldn't answer him back, he screamed and hurled the phone into the air, until it hit and cracked the man in the mirror in his face. The sight of the broken man before him wasn't enough to satisfy Chauncey's anger. He took the phone and struck him again, breaking him a little more than he already was, until the mirror was no more.

Brontae held onto the cigarette in his mouth for dear life. He needed it to last as long as it could because he didn't know what he was going to do next once it was gone. He couldn't stay outside the hotel smoking all night. Despite his predicament, the cigarette didn't last the forever he needed it to.

What exactly his predicament was, was exactly what Brontae was trying to figure out.

He'd seen Malicious Matters have a meltdown, met the only other person who had witnessed it for what it was, and had had the best conversation he'd had in months with someone who thought he was smart and funny. And somewhere in between, he'd fucked up and become someone else, one of the same bitter gays who made the Black gay world that he was beginning to hate as hard as it was. Not knowing how that had happened to him scared him.

Even though he intended to call Justin tomorrow when he, hopefully, wasn't drunk, right now he was. He was also alone. And he was so tired of being alone. Was it just him, he wondered as he followed a flock of other Black gays back inside Hotel Moore, or was the loneliness just part of the Black gay way? Looking at the group of friends, he was curious about whether they longed for intimate companionship in the same way that he did or were they content with just a drunk kiki.

For the moment, they seemed to be content.

"Which one?" he overheard one of them say as they ogled over a passing couple. "Oh, well, I don't know 'bout the bottom, but I wish tha top would come sit on my dick!"

Brontae didn't find either one of the men in the couple cute but he did find himself wondering if their relationship would make it through Black Gay Pride weekend, with all the rampant temptation that was in town.

They'd probably break up by the end of the night, Brontae said to himself as he waited for the elevator.

Once it came, he stepped inside and was immediately greeted by the young gay he shared it with.

"Happy Pride!" he said with all the happiness in the world in his voice.

"Happy Pride," Brontae grumbled, bothered by this young gay's stupid smile and the way he held his head up high and how his eyes were angelically looking up to a heaven he saw and Brontae didn't.

His energy was impenetrable. Brontae's callousness didn't cause a single crease on his face.

It must have been his first Pride or something, Brontae guessed, *because he looked hopeful, and not just hopeful for a few days of non-stop partying. Hopeful for something else.*

For a split-second, Brontae envied his enthusiasm but then the elevator doors closed and he turned to Brontae with his mile-wide smile and said, "Wanna do a bump?"

That's when Brontae realized just how drunk he must have been to make the mistake of forgetting that no one in town this weekend was pure. There were only so many asses to fuck and dicks to suck and everyone was here to see just how many they could in the course of one weekend.

Brontae almost shook his head and declined, but he was so tired of shaking his head. It was easier to just go along with it, all of it, because not doing what everyone else was doing didn't make him any different, he thought. It didn't leave him any less lonely. Tonight had proved that. It was in him too—the tendency to do that thing that Lauryn Hill tried to warn everyone about. Then, drunk and distracted, he thought, *How did that song go, again? "Doo-Wop That Thing?" Was that the name of it?*

"Sure. Why not?" he answered.

Brontae followed the jovial gay to his room where they did exactly two bumps together. When that same jovial gay tugged at his crotch, Brontae let him. When he went down on him, Brontae didn't stop him nor did he ask him if it was okay if he could spray his glob of cum inside his mouth. This lack of permission made his release all the more explosive.

After he unloaded himself, Brontae didn't stop to wonder if the stranger who had sucked him off would swallow his ooze whole or spit it out. He zipped up his pants and left him in his room to decide for himself.

It had all happened so quickly that Lauryn Hill and her song about an unnamed thing that guys and girls better watch out for was still in his head. He hummed the half-remembered melody down the hallway on his way back to the room, fully resigned to the influence he was under, which was no longer just limited to the alcohol. As he approached his door, he sung the song a little louder so he couldn't hear his own thoughts and expectations about what was waiting behind it. But still, he knew that Chauncey would be in there, dressed and ready to go to The Menotaur, no doubt, and do what they always did there, only this time with no LeMilion. His death hadn't changed Chauncey any more than it changed this sick, sad world. It was what it was and would always be.

Brontae allowed himself a second before he opened the door to that inevitability.

But to his surprise, it was nothing like what he'd expected.

The room was in shambles. Everything had been turned upside down. The curtains had been torn from the windows and were on the floor. The paintings no longer hung on the wall. What was breakable was broken, what was tearable was torn, and anything that may have been missed, Chauncey was in the process of wrecking.

Brontae wasn't even sure Chauncey realized he had walked in from the way he went on, drunk, frenzied, crying and naked with little traces of blood on his behind, doing as much damage as he could to the room with no regard to the consequences that would surely be waiting outside of it.

Brontae had no idea what had happened to him and he didn't need one. He only knew that whatever the night had done to his friend was not so unlike what the night had done to him and that was enough. So, with no questions asked, Brontae joined Chauncey in the fight he was in, picking up the alarm clock and throwing it with all the strength he had left in him.

He stood over it, studying its destruction before he stomped it into pieces. He could see the appeal. Satisfaction began to form in his heart. So he went and found his next victim, something of greater weight, the wireless speaker playing the soundtrack to this rampage in the form of an old-school R&B song.

"Bitch, I think the fuck not," Chauncey snapped at him with his eyes red, his face dead serious, and his only concern on the one thing that was in Brontae's hands. "Dat's my fuckin' song."

The way he said it, the playful seriousness in his voice, made them stop and see this moment in a new light. Brontae set the speaker down and let the only thing that apparently mattered to Chauncey play. As the soulful song coming out of the speaker that was somehow still connected to Chauncey's busted cell phone went on, Brontae realized he'd never heard Chauncey listen to old-school R&B before. It was a soothing surprise for him.

The two friends, one of them fully naked and one of them fully clothed, looked at one another. Then they looked at the ridiculous state the room was in and let out a laugh that kept them from crying and made them weak until they had dropped to their knees, laughing over all the damage that had been done.

ABOUT THE AUTHOR

Casey Hamilton is a writer with his roots in raw, fictional storytelling. A native of Baton Rouge, Louisiana, and a graduate of Southern University and A&M College, he now writes from Atlanta, Georgia. After briefly working as a freelance copywriter, Hamilton followed his passion for creative writing with his 2013 amateur debut as a YouTube content creator and star of the gay web series *Judys*.

AMBLE
P R E S S

Amble Press, an imprint of Bywater Books, publishes fiction and narrative nonfiction by LGBTQ writers, with a primary, though not exclusive, focus on LGBTQ writers of color. For more information on our titles, authors, and mission, please visit our website.

www.amblepressbooks.com

CPSIA information can be obtained
at www.ICGtesting.com
Printed in the USA
LVHW030543081021
699881LV00004B/16